THE MECHANICS OF
HOMOSEXUAL INTERCOURSE

THE MECHANICS OF
HOMOSEXUAL INTERCOURSE

STORIES BY
LONELY CHRISTOPHER

LITTLE HOUSE
ON THE BOWERY

AKASHIC BOOKS
NEW YORK

Also from Dennis Cooper's
Little House on the Bowery Series

Cows
by Matthew Stokoe

High Life
by Matthew Stokoe

The Late Work of Margaret Kroftis
by Mark Gluth

The Show that Smells
by Derek McCormack

Userlands: New Fiction Writers from the Blogging Underground
edited by Dennis Cooper

Artificial Light
by James Greer

Wide Eyed
by Trinie Dalton

Godlike
by Richard Hell

The Fall of Heartless Horse
by Martha Kinney

Grab Bag
by Derek McCormack

Headless
by Benjamin Weissman

Victims
by Travis Jeppesen

This is a work of fiction. All names, characters, places, and incidents are the product of the author's imagination. Any resemblance to real events or persons, living or dead, is entirely coincidental.

Published by Akashic Books
©2011 Lonely Christopher

ISBN-13: 978-1-936070-80-0
Library of Congress Control Number: 2010922718

First printing

Little House on the Bowery
c/o Akashic Books
PO Box 1456
New York, NY 10009
info@akashicbooks.com
www.akashicbooks.com

to my parents

THE ORDER

THAT WHICH

Mom said she raised a good boy, a fine son. I am that which she speaks on. I am glad to have been born. It was luck I was born of her and not of a mom that was in a house that was in a part of town far from the mom I did get and love still. I could have been raised up in some place quite bad. I would be dead now. But I have the mom I have. I have her still. She raised me. We used to drive by some of the homes I did not like in our car, mom and me, when the homes still stood, and I would look out at each of them and think on who could be in such a place. We would not stop and go in them. We would go back where we live. I know I am a good boy as mom told me and still says. I know I am in the best place I could be. I do love mom so. I did not care so much for dad. He stayed in his room most days and at night. He would not let me in if I had come to knock for him to say hi. He would not look at me if he could help it. He oft did not care to hear it when I said I loved him, as I had to say to him to be a good boy. I guess he was sad that I got sick. He got lone and blue and full of pain. It was like this since my head broke. I don't know why that is. I can't tell why dad did what he did. I'm not sure why he frowned and would not talk to me when I got my skull took off. I wished he would have changed back to how he used to be. I prayed for it at church when mom drove me there. I don't get why dad had to act like he had got more hurt in him than I had when it is me who fell down. I tried to be real good when it came to all my pain so as not to make mom fret for me. I shoved all the pain hid in my gut where mom can't see it. I kept it thus most of the time. I did not let it out when she was in the same room. I still keep it safe that way these days. Dad did not learn that trick. I wished he learned since I did not want mom to fret for him or me or at all. I told mom I love her and she said it back, of course. I did not quite love dad, and sure did not like him, not the way he was in the end, but I thought it was my job to be nice and the right thing to do was let him know his son loved him all the same, true or not. Oft I dreamed he was the one that which spilt all down the front steps of the house. It could have been him that morn, felled on some ice he did not see when he went out the door. He could have met my fate in place of me. That stone step was loosed on the stairs all the same and if he stepped on it first it would have been his cracked skull and leaked brains and not mine. I'd have liked that, I guess. But it was not to be. I knew then as I still do that that which has been don't change, but yet I dreamt he took that fall and not me. I was so pained and it was so hard to think on what needs done, but I did not let it show like dad did. Dad would act like he had got it worse, though he was not sick from a real fall like mine. I did not know what to think all the time. One time I was a bright boy, mom said, but time came I knew that's gone now, though I'm still her prize, mom said: a good boy, a fine son. I would not frown in front of mom like dad did when he got the chance. That made mom fret to see him do. She could not make him smile like she used to do. Most of the time he did not let her in his room at all, much like how it was he was rude to me. I guess there was once since my bad luck when I saw him for more than a brief pause. He came out of his room for hours the time when he heard me watch a show where two planes flew down and hit a tall house and its twin house in a town I don't know the name of but that which used to be near here. Dad came out and he stood by my chair and looked at the screen. Then he craned his neck and looked at me, like a real look, for a long time for the first time since he put my brains back in place (as the fall spilt them from my crown and on the stairs' stone and a bit on the front yard). Then he quit the look and turned back at the show, which was still on, and he stayed there like that. The plane clip came back and back on this dumb show. It played the same thing more times than I felt it should have. I got bored. I felt like the show ought to change or end. I did not like too much of the same thing. I had no clue what it was in dad that brought him out to watch this show with me, or at least next to me. I did not dare speak lest I drive him off. I watched him though I tried to make it look like I was not. The more he watched the screen the more I saw him change. I saw his face puff up and get wet. His nose turned red like I had not seen it do in the past. His eyes looked like he had pet the cat too much. I did not know what could be wrong, but that was not new when it came to poor dad. I did not ask if I could try to make him less blue since I knew he would not let me help him. He looked worse and worse and did not move. When the sun went down, and the show changed at last, he slunk back to his room with no words to let me know what caused him to act so queer. I did not like how hard it was to have him for my dad, but it could have been worse I guess. It could have been mom who had got my bad luck to spill the way I did that morn. I did not dare to think such a thing: it is so bad. I wish I'd drop dead just to have let it in my head. I could have died that morn. I did think so all the time and there were days I wish I had. When I wished it too much I had to find mom. If she was not there with me I would go to her for help. She oft has a mind for what I can do to be a good boy. I went to her that time when dad watched the show with me and then went back to his room. I found her right when dad was gone and told her what he'd done. She sat me on her lap and fed me some fruit. I was so glad for her love and such a snack as that which she put in my throat. I did not cry but she did cry. I asked if what I'd said of dad made her cry. She pet me and said no, she was just sad for all her friends who had died at work that day, all of them gone in a flash. I did not know what to say to be a good boy then. I failed to do much at all and grew sad too. I was sad I failed, and sad for mom, but mom was sad for her dead friends. We were both glum then and so I wept with her. She tried to dry my tears and I tried to dry hers. She told me that I will be her good boy for all time. I stuck my wet face in her blouse. I pulled a crease in her dress. My lips went near her lips. I was sad but full of thanks too, thanks that I had no friends for I would sure hate to have them all die at once like mom's did. She said I was her last friend in the world, but that was all that a mom like her could need. That stopped my tears. I felt like I had won a hard game and was proud of it. I am still proud to this day and my love for mom is the same or it could be that it has grown. I know that though fate was cruel to me once, there are oft great things to feel in this world, and that is why we keep on with the drudge of our damn lives: that which we find hard here and there is made worth it when you have a mom like my mom to love and to be your best friend. If I was dead now I would not be as near to mom. Plus mom would be lone and drear, left back on this earth when I'd gone. I'd hate to leave her like that and not be there to help. It's such a bad thought it's hard for me to let it in my head, but it would be the same for me if I lived but mom was gone. In that case I would be left back to weep with no mom to hold me and tell me I'm a good boy. I would be here with just dad, which would make it all the worse. He would not cook meals, and I can't as I lack the skills since you know what. In fact, I fear that if mom were gone the both of us left back would starve. I could eat what's left in the fridge for a week or so, if dad did not get to it first, but the food would run out and I would get thin and die. I prayed when I would be at church to make sure this did not come to pass, and to make sure god knows I mean it I told him threats. If mom died and I lived, I would take a plane and fly it down and hit all the homes in the world. If dad died it would all be the same, more or less. I did not wish he'd die, but, as I've said, I would as soon that he had got his skull took off so as to save me from all the pain I feel. It should have been him that morn. Oh, I should not have said that! My wish is true but so dark. It is wrong to dream such things and here I want to be a good boy. I ought not have such bad thoughts so oft when it comes to dad but more so mom! What I meant was that it is as well that it was me who slipped on the patch of ice since dad was old and it did not take much to hurt him quite deep. Had it been him who fell he would not have had the luck I had to save most of my head. Once the cat scratched his arm and he bled and bled on the cloth mom put down for a meal. Dad had not come out to sup with us, which he did not do much, but he was there in the room where we were to eat since he had to feed the pill to the cat (mom could not get it down in way back of the cat's mouth like the vet said it has to go for it to work and I had not the skill for such a task). Dad held the cat and put the pill in her throat and the cat stuck out a hind claw and dug a thin pink line in his arm, the arm that which had a watch on the wrist. There came from that mark a tide of blood that which seemed more than should have been in him at all. The blood spewed from his wound and hit the cloth set out for our sup that night. The white cloth soaked the blood up like a drink. I went to fetch a pad of gauze to mend dad since that is one chore I could do still and not mess up. Dad was sore that the cat scratched him. He spoke, which was rare, and cursed the cat and vowed to make it bleed twice as much as he had just done. I doubt the cat meant real harm since she liked dad and she liked to have her pill. I helped mend his arm with gauze, but he gave me no thanks. He just stormed back to his room in a huff. Mom and me had to fold the soaked cloth, not fit now to have a meal on. I watched her bunch the cloth up and throw it out back with the trash. That was too bad, but it was just one of those things. It was not the cat's fault, but dad blamed her. I caught him when he took it out on her for days with a push or a kick if she went near the door of his room. Mom and me made a plan not to bring it up to dad so it might leave his mind. I don't think it worked. Dad sulked for a long time, but would dart out to punch the cat if she came near when he would creep down the hall to use the john late at night. I kept these things from mom to make her fret less that dad might be worse still. I don't think she had more of a clue than me what made dad act like he did, but she cared more for him than I cared for him and so it made her way more down than me and it was that which I did not like to stand for. I tried to solve her woes for dad but my brain was too bruised and shaped wrong. I lost some skills since you know what and there are some skills I bet I would have grown that I won't get now. That's why it makes it so hard to solve what was wrong with dad. I did not get it! I guess it's just a fact of my tough luck that which makes life hard for me. I used to fear that one day we will all die. I thought that which comes next, when we're dead, should be clear, so I can think, and soft, since mom likes soft things, and I hoped all the pain would be gone so I would not have to hide all of it in my gut when I'm with mom and so dad would be fixed and would act how he used to. I dreamt it would be that way. I know now things will not be the same as I thought in the end. I did not care too much on what death would be like since I knew at least I must be with mom when we die. I thought I would not mind if it's not how I'd like it as long as I'm with mom there. I would not stand for it if we were kept twain in death. I won't be kept from her! I made up my mind that if god kept me from her to fly a plane up and hit god and he would burst out in flames like a house. I warned him when I prayed. I did not tell mom these things so she would not fret. There were days I thought on such things when she was near. We were in the same room once when I did start to think of threats to pray. I tried to make it seem like I did not have much on my mind but she saw me sweat and quake. She asked what was wrong and I did not want to lie to her so I asked to leave the room. I said I felt faint, as I did tend to since the fall. I went off and tried to kill the thoughts that itched my brain. I went and looked out in the yard, that I might see a thing or two to put me at ease. I pressed my face on the glass pane. I pressed hard and dreamt that my face would break through the glass and leave shards in my head to let those thoughts out through the wound holes. The meat in my gut boiled like soup. I could hear dad pace back and forth in his room. I saw a bird in a tree but could not hear it chirp. I thought on how it would be warm soon. It was near the date I had been born on: mom told me she had plans to bake me a cake. She is my best friend. I thought on how I would grow up and mom would give me a gift each year on the day I was born on. I was glad of this and I looked out at the cold lawn and saw the cat stalk by the tall grass at the edge of the yard. I stayed where I was to wait for the sun to slide down in the ground where I could not see it. I heard dad shut the door to his room and stalk down the hall. I got a good way off from the view of the yard. I went back to mom. I told her the whole truth of why I had to leave her side and vowed not to keep things from her. I told her I just did want to have good thoughts when she was near with me. She said it would all be fine in the end, though it was hard for right now. We hugged. I had good thoughts then. I told her that so she would not fret. I stayed pressed as close to her as could be. I felt her touch the lumped flesh of my brow and the deep scars that run down my bald pate. I knew she loved me. Mom stood up, and I nudged off her, and I watched her move to where she kept the knife, by the sink. She picked the knife up and held it like a toy as she looked at it shine in the thread of light from the bulb that which hung near. I smiled and went to the lamp that which sat on the desk at the edge of the room and turned it on. We stood at the ends of the room for a long time, and then mom spoke. Her voice did then sound like the moon when she spoke well of me. She told me I am a good boy and her best friend. She rubbed the knife on her blouse like to wipe a smear off the blade. I think she wept but the tears were too small to see drip down her cheeks from where I was. I wept too, for joy. She asked what bad thoughts had made me sweat and quake. I told her I did not want to say for fear she would think less of me. She asked to give her a clue at least. I looked at her face as she looked at me and then the knife and back at me. I said I had to find a way for me to be with her like this and for us to not grow old and die. Mom smiled and I knew then she meant it when she said it would be fine. She asked if I would like to drive to church right now. She held the knife up in the light. I went from the lamp to where she stood by the sink and leaned on her waist. I wrapped her thighs in a hug. She put her hand on the flat spot of my skull and I felt the cold blade she held rest on my scalp like a kiss. I pressed my face in the folds of her dress, breathed in a gulp of her smell, and felt my lungs go limp. We would take a ride to church, just the two of us, like we liked. It pleased me so much, our plan, as I tried to squeeze my arms more tight to hold her and not let go. My tears made a sink in her dress. I cried at her waist and asked for the thing that which I knew I must hear from her. I asked her to tell me that we would not be wrought twain by death. I did not care if god did not want it to be the truth, I knew it would be made true if mom said it. Her voice would drown out god and save our love. My nerves winced and my pain burst from where I had it hid in my gut and all my bones turned to jam and my tongue to salt. It was from the wait for mom's voice since it did not come as quick as I'd hoped. I tried to look up, to beg her, but her hand that which grasped the knife was pressed down on me too hard. I feared to break the pause but I could not help it. I could not stop the blurt that which came out of my stung throat that which had the sound of a cough made of salt, but was in fact my way to let mom know that I love her and our love is the gift that which makes it worth such pain as that which pumps my blood through my heart so I might live. And it was all fine: she was right. I had to wait for time to end to hear her voice, but when her mouth went wide she sang. Till then we had not once moved, nor made no sounds, but we watched the rest of what there is run out and we saw all the planes fall from the sky and the homes turn back to dirt. We stood there till life on earth was gone,

and death was gone, and that which was left was all ours, at
last.

THE MECHANICS OF
HOMOSEXUAL INTERCOURSE

♥♥♥

The calico couch was not where it had been a few months previous. Morton stood and examined his living room; his son Dumb sat inattentive in a chair that needed to be relocated. "How was it?" Morton asked of the general arrangement. The couch was against the wall with the windows that looked out onto the street, but presently Morton approached it and began to push it toward the space where the piano was. The chair Dumb sat in was by the door that led into the dining room but it used to be by the door that led into the entryway. "Help me out here," Morton implored, nudging the couch closer to its old place. "I don't want to move the piano," Dumb sighed. "But it used to be by the window and the couch was there," said Morton. Dumb helped move the piano slightly. "It still isn't completely accurate," Morton said. The piano was only halfway to the window and the coffee table was obstructing the door to the dining room. "It doesn't matter," said Dumb. "Let's see," said Morton, "you were sitting on the couch with me. This lamp was—oh this is a new lamp! Let's put this in the other room. I think that one chair was by the other door." Dumb moved the chair while his father supervised. Dumb sat down in the chair after it had been moved. "No, sit on the couch," said Morton. "Right was sitting at the piano." Morton adjusted the piano bench. "We'll pretend it's where it really should be for now, it's rather heavy," he said. Dumb stood up and walked to the calico couch and sat on it. "Right was here," Morton said, sitting down at the piano, "and he sort of pawed at the keys every now and again and looked over at you. Move a little to the other side, please Dumb. Yes, now he was sitting here giving you little looks and, well, I remember he said, 'There were two kids who were going to a shitty little high school somewhere stupid. And the first kid came up to the second kid in the hallway in the middle of the school day, it was Valentine's Day, and asked the second kid to be his Valentine. The second kid didn't like that very much because he didn't like that some queer like the first kid could think *he* would ever have anything to do with a *boy* when there were so many cheerleaders around with nice tits. And the second kid liked fucking tits. And he hated faggots. So what the second kid did was he went home and the next day he brought his dad's Glock with him to school, found the first kid in the hallway, and when the first kid turned around and saw who it was and gave him a loving look, the second kid fired a bullet into the first kid's neck. And he died.' That's what he said, or that's an approximation. I suppose I was drinking wine." Dumb looked at his father. "Are we done?" he asked. "No!" said Morton. "We have to reconstruct the event more fully." Dumb scratched his leg. "But it doesn't matter," he said, "because Right killed himself." Morton stood up and attempted to nudge the piano in the proper direction. "That's precisely why it *does* matter," he told his son. Dumb tried to think about that then he scratched his leg again. "Mom told me her boyfriend in college died in a drunk driving accident," said Dumb. Morton sat down beside him on the calico couch and caught his breath. "I know that," he said, "it's how I met her." Dumb didn't look at his father. "Everyone dies," he offered. "Don't change the subject," said Morton. "Why are we doing this?" asked Dumb. "To recreate the circumstances in which your relationship with Right ended so as to better understand his untimely death," said Morton. "It's a great technique, very effectual." "Well," said Dumb, "he sat at the piano, he gave me little looks, he said mean things, he ended up having one of his seizures . . ." "That's right!" Morton said. "Then a few weeks later he was dead," Dumb concluded. Morton shook his head. "This is going to take more time," he said, "but you're certainly not going to benefit from summarizing like that, and skipping ahead so far." Dumb was bored. He tried to discover feelings of sadness but that only confused him so he didn't say anything. "We can start with general questions," Morton suggested. "Why did he have seizures?" "It was a medical condition," Dumb replied. "What caused him to have an episode during the specific incident we are investigating?" asked Morton. Dumb tried to think of an answer until he had too much to say, so he didn't bother.

♥♥♥

Some nights Morton would exit his study holding an empty wine bottle and pause in front of his son's room on the way to bed, and he would think of what might be happening on the other side of the door between Dumb and his boyfriend Right, but when Right died Morton could only imagine his lonely son sitting and reading a book, and he knew there would be no more curiosity unless there was another boy. Morton left his study holding an empty wine bottle and a book he was unready to set down, and passed his son's closed bedroom door without pausing. Dumb sat at his desk and looked into his lamp until his eyes hurt, then he shone the lamp back down on the surface of his desk where he had made several lines of powder from a pill he had crushed up. Dumb sniffed the powder using a piece of a straw and then listened to Glenn Gould playing the *Goldberg Variations* on his laptop. He moved from his desk to his bed, and picked up a book, and thought of what the book was about, then he read the book, and thought of Right. Right sat in the corner of Dumb's room, never on the bed unless they were fucking or sleeping together, and read books with serious titles, and frowned, and interrupted Dumb's concentration with endless philosophical lectures, entirely cynical and dense; Dumb tried to listen to him even when he wasn't trying to be coherent, contradicting himself as he made a convoluted argument, and then one day he wasn't alive, but Dumb was alive, and Dumb stayed in his room, on his bed, holding a book and listening to Glenn Gould. "I'm only pretending to like you," said Right, "because I get so bored." "Okay," said Dumb. "The only thing I care about is nihilism," said Right. "That's kind of cute," said Dumb. "I know," said Right, "I hate it!" Dumb would revisit a little memory when he wasn't thinking enough about anything different, but he couldn't be sentimental about that. It made him feel less.

♥♥♥

The apartment was in one of two long fat buildings that ran the length of the block, separated by a dreary gulch of a street littered with crushed beer cans. Both buildings were previously purposed for industrial use and were not zoned residentially, but they were filled with unfinished loft apartments, one of which was particularly crowded on a woolly night with kids nearly pressed up against each other, holding beers and talking loudly. Dumb was there with his girlfriend Lucy, and they stood in the corner of the loft next to a dirty stove, holding bottles of beer noncommittally and trying to squint out into the dense congregation of kids all around them. "I don't think we know anyone," Dumb told Lucy. "I think we know somebody on the other side of the room," said Lucy. "Well I hope they're having fun over there," said Dumb. Lucy rested her head on his shoulder. "We'll never know how much more fun it is on the other side of the room," she said. Dumb barely heard her because of the racket of voices. Nearby, a smiling kid was being given a birthday cake with twenty-one candles burning on top of it. "Happy birthday!" said the people around him. Dumb touched Lucy's head, and then he tried to move. He squeezed through the small spaces between people standing close together until he reached one of the giant windows that looked out onto the street. There was a fire truck parked down the block; its flashing lights colored the façades of both buildings. Firemen in black uniforms ran from door to door, carrying axes, trying to get into the building opposite the one Dumb was in. Dumb turned away and made it back to where Lucy stood. "I wonder if any of these people are interesting," said Dumb. "They don't look interesting," said Lucy, "they all look like art students." Dumb drank his beer. "I guess none of us has anything better to do," said Dumb. "I could be editing Wikipedia," said Lucy. "I like being here with all these kids doing nothing and I don't know any of them," said Dumb. "A boy just walked up to you and is standing behind you, looking at you," said Lucy. Dumb turned around and saw the boy. "Hi?" said Dumb. "I saw you and I thought I could probably talk to you," said the boy. "Oh! We're drunk," said Dumb. The boy drank from the beer he was holding. "Well hello in that case," said Dumb. "My name is Orange," said the boy. "I'm

Dumb," Dumb said. "What's up?" asked Orange. "Are you an art student?" asked Dumb. "Yes," said Orange. "Where did you come from?" asked Dumb. Orange pointed behind him. "The other side of the room," he said. "You must be so brave to have traveled all this way!" said Dumb. Orange shrugged. "I wanted to talk to you," he said. "Why?" asked Dumb. "Are you queer?" asked Orange. "Yes," said Dumb. "Brilliant," Orange said. Dumb introduced Orange to Lucy. "This is my girlfriend," he said. "Hello," Orange said. "I'm going to try and get in line for the bathroom," said Lucy, and she squeezed between two people and disappeared. "Do you like Andy Warhol?" asked Orange.

♥♥♥

Dumb and Orange sat together at a small table in a café in the city, drinking coffee. "This is going better than I thought," said Orange. "Oh, good," said Dumb. "You seem sort of reserved and standoffish at times, but you're very gentle," said Orange. "Your teeth are very clean and bright," said Dumb. "I guess we were made to be together," said Orange. Dumb occupied himself with his coffee. "Do you have a boyfriend?" asked Dumb. "Not really. A few. I don't know," said Orange. Dumb smiled. "Do you?" asked Orange. "No, I'm on the *rebound*," said Dumb. "Great," said Orange. "My last boyfriend killed himself," Dumb said. "Oh," said Orange. "It wasn't my fault or anything—he was sort of distraught . . . or terminally frustrated," said Dumb. "He was an intellectual, huh?" said Orange. "He was a philosopher king in his head, at least. Let's make the rest of our informal date about my boyfriend who is dead," said Dumb, "ex-boyfriend, I mean." Right did not like having seizures in public, it ashamed him; and since there was so much in public that could inspire him to a seizure, he did not often go out with Dumb, and never to the city, where the people he found most intolerable, whose behavior was most likely to unknowingly drive Right into a state of disgust that would turn into a seizure, came together to meet each other in small cafés or to sit in bars downtown. "And there are too many faggots in the city downtown," said Right. "There are fags, poetasters, and jejune cretins everywhere! They make them at these universities." When Dumb tried to kiss him he would frown; Dumb had to wait until he was distracted for a moment of reciprocity in a kiss Dumb initiated before Right would realize how his immediate reaction to the kiss belied his dislike of tender gestures. Finally his body was gone and probably nobody got to touch it, which would have met his approval. "I wonder if anybody changes, whatever," said Dumb. He looked into his cup, then at his date. Dumb moved his leg so that it was touching Orange's leg under the table. "Your dead boyfriend is a prick for killing himself. If I can say that," said Orange. "He could be like a diva, I guess, and, um, messianic? He'd kill me for saying that, because it's the wrong word. He was really frustrated about being smarter than me," Dumb shrugged. "I try to read a lot," he added, "but he always read more, it's all he did besides talk about the void and admonish me for being facile." "You should think about something else," said Orange, "like me." Dumb said, "And will you think about me, then?" They kept talking and sipping coffee. As the night arrived Orange saw the street grow darker through the window behind Dumb. "We should go to the park," said Orange. "Great," said Dumb. When they finished their coffee, and paid for it, they left. The park was mostly empty except for an idling police car and those who were using the dog run. Orange looked at trees. "This would be fun to draw," he said, touching a mangled one. Dumb stood still, looked at the tree, and Orange leaned on him. Orange leaned his head on Dumb's shoulder and they stood that way in silence. Then Orange said, "Can I do something forward?" Dumb said, "What?" Orange kissed him. "Oh!" said Dumb. Orange blushed. They walked to a bench, and sat down, and held hands, watching the animals play in the dog run. Orange brought his face to Dumb's face, and they kissed again, and that, and other things like that, happened several more times as they sat on the bench in the park, not saying much, until finally Orange had to go to the bathroom. When Dumb stood up he realized he had an erection. They walked to a bar nearby and Orange slipped into the bathroom while Dumb looked around and almost tried to order a drink. When they left the bar they went back to the park and kissed again.

♥♥♥

The calico couch was where it was before it had been moved back to where it was several months previous and the new lamp was sitting on the coffee table by the chair. Morton and his wife Alice were seated on the couch, perusing two typed copies of a manuscript, when Dumb walked into the living room from the entryway. "You're back finally!" Morton exclaimed when he saw his son. "What is it?" asked Dumb. "Please, take a seat," said Morton. Dumb obeyed suspiciously. "I want to try a new approach," said Morton, "that I think will be very therapeutic." "Oh," said Dumb. Morton waved the manuscript he was holding in the air. "I have crafted a *dramatic scenario* in which you and Right are the characters interacting, with dialogue that I believe maintains a suitable fidelity to the actual language of your conversations insofar as I knew them, and pertinent topics, videlicet interpersonal relationships and dealing with depression, are addressed in such a way that hopefully you will be able to perceive the circumstances surrounding Right's death and the consequent end of your romantic involvement with him from a previously unconsidered perspective that nourishes your emotional faculties and helps you process the change that death of a loved one brings," he said. "Well, okay," Dumb said. "I'll be playing the role of Right," said Morton, "and your mother will be playing the role of Dumb." Dumb nodded. "Remember the notes on line delivery I gave you," Morton whispered to Alice, "and we're not reading the stage directions this time." Alice nodded. "I love you," she said. Morton cleared his throat. "How can you say that, how can you *feel* that, when right now there's a sixteen-year-old pregnant girl getting raped with a knife by her father somewhere! It's absolutely sophomoric," said Morton. "But we're sophomores," said Alice. "You're not stupid, so I don't know what you're doing wasting your time convincing yourself you love people," said Morton. "It just happens," Alice said. "It's a sociopolitical hallucination," said Morton, "and I disrespect you for valuing it so much." "I'm sorry, I can't help it," said Alice. "No, you can too help it but you don't because you're under the delusion that *love* will make things better, or will redeem your meaningless life, imbue it with some sort of contrived resonance," said Morton. "It's a feeling not an ideology," said Alice. "Then why do you try to predicate your understanding of your surroundings on it?" asked Morton. "Why do you attack me when I just want to be close to you?" asked Alice. "Because your spatial praxis is fucked," said Morton. "At least I don't use pedagogic despair as an excuse to be so hateful," said Alice. "We'll never escape the binary, will we? You *love* and I *hate*, it's as uncomplicated as that for you all the time, isn't it?" Morton asked. "I'm not the one who killed himself," said Alice. "I was bored," said

Morton. "You were depressed because you were so insecure. All you wanted was ambiguity, but it prevented you from accepting the love I offered, and the struggle of denial became so difficult you made a desperate decision out of weakness to kill yourself so you didn't have to face your problems," said Alice. "I'm not weak," said Morton. "You're not here," said Alice, "and the only thing I can do is learn and grow from my experience with you, because I understand now you weren't being theoretical, you were just scared." Morton and Alice both put down their manuscripts, and Dumb felt pressured to applaud them briefly. "Oh, thank you," Alice smiled. "I hope the ending wasn't too bluff," said Morton, "but you get the gist, I think." Dumb stood up. "Do you want to have a discussion about your reaction now or after you've had some time to digest it?" said Morton. "Um," said Dumb, "in a while." "Very good then," said Morton, and he leaned over and hugged his wife. "I think that went well," said Alice. "Decidedly so," said Morton. Dumb went to his room and closed the door behind him. He took a pill out of a bottle he kept in a drawer, sat down at his desk, and crushed the pill into a powder, then made several lines and sniffed them with a piece of a straw. He thought about Right having a seizure on his floor, and trying to resist when Dumb held him, but not being able to control anything as he shook. Dumb played Glenn Gould on his laptop and sat looking into his lamp until his eyes hurt, then he turned the lamp away.

♥♥♥

Walter was an older cousin of Dumb's; a thin effeminate man who lived in the city in a small apartment far uptown, and his impending marriage to his lover Nicholas became the source of much excitement and preparation as the date of the ceremony drew nearer. Walter was beholden to Morton, who contributed an undisclosed sum to partly fund the wedding, and so he felt obligated to always accept the invitations to dinner that Morton enthusiastically extended to him and his fiancé. One night the couple was a guest of the household and everyone sat around the dining room table as Alice brought in dishes of food from the kitchen. "Did you ever resolve the issue with the cake?" asked Morton. "Oh!" said Walter. "We took a bath on that awful bakery—they are just a bunch of scam artists. Now we're basically back to square one with the cake." Nicholas shook his head in frustration. He said, "We were better off when none of this was allowed." Walter touched the back of his fiancé's neck. "Nicholas is just a wreck this week, but he knows there's nobody better than the likes of us to put on a show in style. We're not worried about the cake." "Can you believe that when Morton and I married we just eloped!" said Alice. "We thought we were being progressive, but we were really just trying to alienate our parents," Morton commented, pouring a glass of wine. "I suppose that's what we're doing too, in a way," said Walter. "Oh, you know your father is very proud of you," said Morton, "he just has a hard time communicating his feelings." "Or lending any support," muttered Nicholas. "Oh stop that," Walter said to his fiancé. "We're lucky for what we have." "Let me know if you run into any more snags," said Morton. "We're doing fine considering the time crunch," said Walter. "The cake is, well, we're going to fix the cake problem, don't fret." "Oh, Dumb," said Nicholas, "be sure to let us know who you're bringing so we can finalize the seating arrangement at the reception." Dumb thought about it. "I'm bringing my friend Lucy and I think my friend Orange," he said. "Yes, Alice and I recently met this boy Orange," said Morton. "It's a very positive step."

"Oh!" said Walter. "Dumb is bringing his girlfriend *and* his boyfriend. I remember when you were five years old, Dumb." Dumb smiled. He tried thinking about what it was like to be five years old. "That's funny," he said.

♥♥♥

The door to Morton's study swung open; Morton walked out into the hallway holding an empty wine bottle. On the way to bed he paused in front of Dumb's closed bedroom door and considered what might be happening on the other side. He knew his son was in there with Orange. He thought about this quietly, presently walked on, and was soon asleep next to his wife. In Dumb's bedroom Dumb was laying in bed holding Orange, and they began to take off each other's clothes. Dumb and Orange didn't have much to say, and so they tried to touch and kiss instead, and they liked it. They took off each other's clothes for a while, and then stopped, and Orange retrieved his sketchbook and began to draw Dumb, but Dumb couldn't sit still. Dumb moved to his desk, and changed the music playing on his laptop, and took out his pills, and crushed one into a powder. "You shouldn't do that!" said Orange from the bed, with his sketchbook in his lap. "Oh," said Dumb. He thought about this. "Why not?" he asked finally. "I don't know," said Orange. "Is it bad?" asked Dumb. Orange shrugged his naked shoulders. "Yes," he said. Dumb divided the powder into lines and sniffed it with a piece of a straw. "Now sit still," said Orange, looking at him. Dumb moved to the bed. He touched Orange's leg. "I'm going to take your underwear off," said Dumb. Orange leaned over his sketchbook and kissed Dumb. Orange smelled Dumb's body. "I like you a lot," said Dumb. He thought about a reason for it, but couldn't find one. "Thanks," said Orange. "I mean I like being close to you," said Dumb. He took off Orange's underwear and saw his cock. "I know that," said Orange. "Have you ever been in love?" asked Dumb. "No," said Orange. "Have you?" Orange took off Dumb's underwear. "I don't think so," said Dumb. He wanted to keep talking about it, but didn't. Dumb put Orange's cock in his mouth. Dumb thought he might be telling a story through the mechanics of intercourse, the knowledge of which had always belonged to him and every other boy he had done this with. He couldn't imagine what kind of story it was, but he didn't care. He thought it was boring but necessary, and since it was necessary it had to be fascinating. So it kept happening, the motions kept becoming actions. Dumb and Orange were naked, they touched, they kissed, eventually Orange asked, "Do you want to have sex?" Dumb thought about it while Orange found a condom and the lubricant. Dumb put a pillow under the small of his back, looked at Orange, put one leg on his shoulder. As they fucked he felt Orange's cock, he looked at the expressions on Orange's face, and after a while both of them came, then Orange took the condom off and put it in the trash bin, and Dumb wiped his ejaculate off his stomach. "Can I fuck you in a while?" Dumb asked. "I'm not sure," Orange said, lying down again. "Oh," said Dumb. "I don't feel like it, actually," said Orange. Dumb didn't say anything. They lay in bed together, and Orange fell asleep, and started to twitch and snore, and then Dumb gently untangled himself from Orange, and stood up, put on his underwear, and sat down at his desk. He smelled the air. He thought about what it must feel like to commit suicide, like sometimes when he thought about the few seconds of life experienced in a car crash between the impact and death, and what would happen then. He tried to pretend that he was Right, having a seizure, but he couldn't. Then he tried to pretend he was Orange, or his father, or his mother, but he couldn't, so he picked up a book from his desk. Dumb was asleep when Orange woke up.

♥♥♥

The streets were wet, and the cars drove through puddles that splashed muddy water onto the sidewalks, but the sky had cleared, and it was sunny now, not raining. Dumb walked with his cousin Walter in the city. They passed many people moving quickly, holding closed umbrellas. "I cannot thank you enough," said Walter, "for coming along with me. That man makes me so nervous!" "It's no problem, really," said Dumb. "Nicholas says thanks too. He was *supposed* to come with and do all the talking, but of course he scheduled an appointment with the florist at the same time. We're really getting down to the wire. Any little bit of help counts," said Walter. They stopped and waited to cross the street. Dumb tapped his closed umbrella on a street sign. "It's fine," he said. "Where do you want to get lunch?" asked Walter. "I don't care," said Dumb. "No really, pick!" said Walter. "It's my treat." "I don't know this neighborhood," said Dumb. "Oh well then," said Walter, "we'll walk a few blocks. There's a French African place you'll adore with a nice champagne brunch I don't think we're too late for." Dumb smiled. People began to cross the street in a crowd, but Walter didn't notice. He wasn't looking at anything, suddenly. "It's hard to get married," he said. Dumb looked at him. "Oh!" Walter said. "I'm sorry." He crossed the street and Dumb followed. Walter laughed, "You'll understand some day." "I don't know," said Dumb. "Don't know what?" asked Walter. "If I like the idea of marriage," Dumb answered. "I mean, personally." Walter smiled, "A holdout, huh? Sticking to the *old way*?" "Well I'm not very political," said Dumb. "All queers are born political, darling," said Walter. "Everything you do is a political statement!" Dumb said, "I'm not certain what I think about that." "Here it is!" said Walter. He held the door of the restaurant open for Dumb. "Of course, if things weren't so *uncertain,* life would be a real drag!" Walter said as they went inside. "Except I wish we could get the cake figured out," he added. They sat down, and the waiter came, and they placed their orders, and the champagne came, and then the food arrived. "So tell me about this new boyfriend of yours," said Walter. "He's not really my boyfriend," said Dumb. "You kids these days are so *sensitive* about labels," Walter replied. "I know my dad told you he was my boyfriend," said Dumb. Walter leaned over his salad. "Your dad . . . well, you know, he's *your dad.* He's been awfully worried about you, and I don't blame him." "I'm fine," said Dumb. "I know," Walter replied, "and you're dating again, or *whatever* you want to call it, and Morton has a lot of enthusiasm for your wellness." Dumb drank all of his champagne. "I don't know if we actually like each other," said Dumb. "Don't be silly," said Walter, "your father loves you!" "No, I mean my boyfriend and me, or whatever," said Dumb. "Oh, of course," said Walter. "Well, uh, I'm sorry if that's the case. Just keep your chin up." "I don't think it matters," said Dumb.

♥♥♥

A faint light came through the blinds when Dumb woke up in bed with his girlfriend Lucy. He saw she was still wearing her glasses and removed them from her sleeping face, setting them aside on the nightstand. When he sat up his clothes felt heavy. He looked for his shoes, but didn't see them. At first he didn't notice he was in significant pain, but then he did. He stood up and walked to the bathroom, where he sat on the edge of the tub and vomited into the toilet. He noticed there was vomit in the little trash bin by the tub. He vomited again until he was only coughing. His body shook for a while and he fell into the tub. He thought for a moment he was having a seizure. Presently Lucy came into the bathroom and looked at him, then she flushed the toilet. She put the seat down, lowered her pants, and sat on it. "Don't pee in front of me," Dumb coughed. "What's wrong with you?" asked Lucy. "I'm not used to drinking so much vodka," said Dumb. "Oh yeah, you said that," said Lucy, "when you were puking in the waste-basket." She wiped herself and got up from the toilet. "I guess I don't have anything better to do," said Dumb. "We could be learning something or something," said Lucy. Dumb tried to get out of the tub, but dramatically collapsed again. "You should take a bath," said Lucy. "This is so silly!" Dumb tried to yell. "You sound terrible," said Lucy. "I need . . . water," said Dumb. Lucy left the room, returning with a glass of ice water. "Was last night cathartic at least?" asked Lucy. "I don't really remember exactly—what happened?" asked Dumb. "I just listened to your problems for like six hours," Lucy replied. Dumb rested the cup against his face. "Oh, but that's what my dad is for," said Dumb. "I know," said Lucy. "Did I say anything stupid?" asked Dumb. "Nothing new," Lucy said. She felt his face and looked at him, then she stood up. "I have to get ready and go to work," she said, "but you can stay here, whatever. Just make sure the door is locked when you leave." In Lucy's absence Dumb didn't think about time, but he finally managed to crawl out of the tub and reach a seat at the kitchen table. Lucy's roommate woke up and left, only saying, "Oh, hi," to Dumb as she passed him. As Dumb prepared to stand up and walk, he watched the light change. It was almost dusk when he left the apartment, stepping out onto the sidewalk and appreciating the breeze. He began to lumber slowly down the street toward the subway. He paid for a ticket in quarters, and then rested on the filthy platform waiting for the train. He thought of little and said nothing. A police officer grimaced at him as she walked by. The train arrived. Dumb managed to stand up and board the train just before the doors closed. He fell down into a seat across from the boy Right, who wasn't looking at him.

♥♥♥

Dumb sat anxiously in the tub, Morton, having lowered the cover, sat on the toilet, and Lucy stood in the doorway of her bathroom holding a beer. "What then?" asked Morton. "Then he said, 'I don't usually drink vodka,' and I told him he told me that when he was puking in the wastebasket before he passed out," said Lucy. "Uh, yeah," Dumb agreed. "And describe how you felt for me, please," said Morton. "Nothing, I guess," said Dumb. "Everything really hurt, and maybe there was only room for some thoughts about what a bad idea it was to have drunk that much." "He asked for water, and I gave it to him, and he drank it, and I told him I had to go to work," said Lucy. Morton turned to her. "Did you leave him here in the tub?" he asked. "I told him to take a bath," she said. "Okay," Morton turned back to his son, "and then what?" "It took me a long time to get out of the tub," said Dumb, standing up, "and then I went out into the kitchen and sat at the table." Dumb walked out; Morton stood and followed along with Lucy. Dumb sat down at the kitchen table as his father looked on. "I sat here for a long time," said Dumb. "Why did you want to drink so much?" asked Morton. "I don't know," said Dumb. "He was sad," Lucy offered. Morton turned to her, "About what?" She said, "Boys and sex and stuff. We had girl talk." Morton frowned. He turned back to his son, "What's the matter?" Dumb was looking only at the table. "Nothing more than usual," he said. "How long did you sit there?" Morton asked. "I don't know, I lost track of time," said Dumb, "but it was just getting dark when I left." "You just sat there doing nothing all day?" asked Morton. "Gathering strength," said Dumb. "Were you thinking about anything in particular?" asked Morton. "Getting into bed," said Dumb. The father and his son continued the investigation until, having thanked Lucy for her help, they left the apartment and finally stood on the platform of the subway station waiting for the train. "How long did it take?" asked Morton. "Maybe fifteen minutes," said Dumb. "I sat over here on the floor." A train arrived and they both boarded it. "Okay, now what side did you sit down on?" asked Morton. "This side, right where that lady is," said Dumb. He pointed to a drowsy woman in a security uniform. Morton approached her. "Excuse me, miss?" he asked. She opened her eyes tentatively. "I'm sorry, but I'm a certified specialist and I'm carrying out a very important therapeutic reenactment activity, and I was wondering if it wouldn't trouble you too much to relocate from that seat." The woman frowned. "I ain't moving," she said. "I apologize for the inconvenience, miss, I really do, but I am going to have to insist that you move. I have two PhDs." The woman grumbled, but she picked up her bag and stood, attempting to reseat herself directly across the car. "Oh! I'm deeply sorry, but I fear we're going to need this one too," Morton said, throwing himself into her intended seat. He leaned around the woman and looked at Dumb, "This *is* where you say you saw . . . him, correct?" Dumb nodded. The woman scowled and moved to the end of the car. "This seat okay?" she yelled, pointing to the spot furthest away from Morton. "That's excellent," Morton replied. "Thank you for your cooperation!"

Dumb sat down across from his father. "I sat down," he said, "and when I looked up . . . the first thing I saw was him." He looked at his father. "Just sitting here?" Morton asked. "He looked preoccupied," said Dumb. "Not noticing you at first," said Morton. "No," said Dumb. Morton continued, "But then, what? He turned . . . and you made eye contact." Dumb sat unmoving. "Yes," he said. "And did he say anything?" asked Morton. "No," said Dumb. "Did you say anything?" asked Morton. "I know it was him," said Dumb. "It was." Morton asked, "What happened?" The train pulled into the next station, stopped, and the doors opened. Morton turned around and observed the platform through the plastic window. "He stood up and got off at this stop," said Dumb. "What did you do?" asked Morton. The doors closed and the train started to move again. "I tried to say something, I don't know," said Dumb. "I tried to stand up, but I wasn't fast enough." Morton looked at his son. "And that was that, then," he said. "It really was him," said Dumb. "This is worse than I thought," said Morton. "I'm afraid you've had a complete relapse if not an entirely new breakdown altogether." "I feel okay," said Dumb. When they exited the subway, they made the short walk to the house without saying much. Finally Morton spoke, "It wasn't necessarily a psychotic hallucination; I won't jump to conclusions until we've talked about it more. We need to discuss the conditions that led to you behaving in such a self-destructive fashion, drinking hard liquor when you aren't accustomed to it, and the depression and immobility you were experiencing before you claim to have seen, in a subway car, a person who is most definitely deceased." Dumb didn't say anything. Morton looked at his son, then he looked at the ground as he walked. He cleared his throat and said, "Son, I'm, well, I'm *sorry*—" "There he is standing outside of our house," said Dumb. Morton looked up. Right was slouched against the railing of the stoop. "What the fuck?" asked Morton.

♥♥♥

The bedroom was unchanged from when Right was alive. Dumb sat at his desk, deciding what music to play on his laptop. "Do you still like Glenn Gould?" he asked Right. Right stood in front of the closed door, staring at it as if looking through it. "Your dad is standing directly on the other side of the door," he said. "I'm afraid we're just going to have to ignore that," Dumb said. He selected a rendition of *The Art of the Fugue* on piano and it began to play. Right turned away from the door and walked to the bed, stood in front of it for a long time, then sat deliberately on the edge of it. He looked at the carpet. "This interpretation has been highly criticized, you know," he said. "I like to hear him humming," said Dumb, still facing his laptop. "Are you *still* so plebeian?" asked Right. "I think it's comforting," said Dumb. Right didn't say anything. Dumb turned around. "You killed yourself," he said. Right almost looked guilty, but quickly defensive. "Nobody really kills himself," he said. "Yes they do," said Dumb, "people do that all the time." "Well they're losers," said Right. "I haven't met them. I'm a genius—did you know that? You probably did know. I think I always knew too. It's peaceful to finally accept." Dumb looked at him for a long time. "I don't think it matters that you're not alive," he said. "Please stop being so obtuse!" said Right. "You must know how irritating I find it." "I'm not the one who died and won't admit it," said Dumb. He stood up, moved his chair closer to the bed, and sat down again. They looked at each other. Dumb reached over and poked Right in the ribs. "Ow!" he said. "Why are you here? What are you doing?" asked Dumb. Right sighed theatrically.

"I don't know; I don't want to think about it," he said. "What does it feel like to kill yourself?" asked Dumb. "It's frightening," said Right. "Something inside of you just turns into the largest possible diamond of awareness, exactly before you die, and it's so sharp it cuts the fabric of your being into little shards, which rain down upon an unknown universe, slicing wounds that blossom into incomprehensible ruptures as they fall." "Oh," said Dumb, "that sounds nice." "I could be making it up, of course," said Right. "Why are you always such a fucking asshole?" asked Dumb. Right reclined on the bed. "It just seemed, intellectually, like the only possible reaction to anything," he said. "But I loved you and that was different," said Dumb. "No," said Right, "it was the same. Same as everything else." "I'm glad I loved you," said Dumb. "I'm glad you did too, to be honest," Right replied. He looked at the ceiling. "But I'm also thankful you had the sense to die," said Dumb. Right leaned over and peered at Dumb. "I would have expected you to be heartbroken," he said. "I think it worked out well for me, actually," said Dumb. "Well I didn't do it for *you*," said Right, "and I benefited immensely from it also." Dumb said, "You seem about the same." Right sat up and folded his legs. "Oh no! I guess you never were very observant. I've made leaps and bounds and it shows. I've come to terms with my asexuality. I don't love or desire anyone. I'm a neuter. That's brought a lot into perspective. And I've been very monastic. I have a hermitage. I think I'm more spiritual now. My philosophical project has definitely shifted focus from nihility to absolute emptiness. Not that you'd know the difference, but it's really changed the game for me. I'm more focused. I rarely have the seizures anymore. Killing myself, as you insist upon calling what I did, really worked out, as a matter of fact." "I've been seeing somebody," said Dumb. Right smiled, "Good for you." Dumb leaned backward in his chair. "I don't know if we're really seeing each other anymore," he said. "He was accessible, but uninteresting." "Aha!" Right said. "All I want is somebody I want to be around and I've never met anyone like that," Dumb said. "You were sort of close, but you were a misanthrope who treated me badly." Right frowned and said, "I hate to rob you of your pathetic hopes, but you're never going to be happy. You're never going to find anyone to make you happy in all the ways you want and think you need. You can't allow that misdirected desire centrality unless you want to be a disappointed ninny forever." Dumb thought about this. He leaned back in his chair again. "Are you sure?" he asked. Right didn't say anything. He walked to the bookshelf, picked out a book he had once lent Dumb, and returned to the bed. "My cousin is homosexual," said Dumb. "You're considering incest?" asked Right, looking at the book. "No," said Dumb, "he's getting married. He's sustaining a loving relationship." Right threw the book down. "Oh *fuck*—of all the stupid, heteronormative, autonomy robbing, hegemonic systems a faggot can submit to in this world, he's going to get *married*! I can't believe you're still related to that cocksucker if he's trying to pull shit like that." "Anyway," said Dumb, "are you going to be around in three weeks?" Right thought about it. "I'm always around, but never available. Or I'm never around, but always available. I'm not sure which one." "Well," said Dumb, "you can come to the wedding with me. Lucy's going to be there, but the boy I invited doesn't want to go." Right stood up, and stretched, and stared at the door. "I don't blame him," he said. "But you're coming," said Dumb. Right didn't answer. "I don't think you're a genius," said Dumb, "I think you're the sorriest retard I know."

♥♥♥

The small cathedral was crowded with friends and relatives for the ceremony. Morton and Alice sat in the front pew next to Walter's father, a widower, whose visible reaction to the event he was witnessing vacillated between disbelief and pride. "I never thought it would be like this," he muttered, overheard by some nearby. Right scowled, but could say nothing. Dumb had never seen Right dressed formally before but thought he looked handsome and healthy despite his suicide. Lucy sat in between the two boys, holding Dumb's hand. Walter and Nicholas stood together, in front of everyone, led through vague and familiar rituals by a wrinkled priest. Both men were teary when they read their personal vows to one another. Soon it was declared that they were officially married. They kissed, marched down the aisle of the small cathedral, and out of the church through a large set of red doors, followed closely by the crowd, which paraded down the front steps cheering, before dispersing in the street to travel to the reception. As Dumb walked down the steps with his two friends, he asked Right, "What do you think?" Right watched the newlywed couple holding hands, posing for photographs before entering an awaiting limousine. "I guess it's like anything else," he replied. "You're in a good mood!" said Dumb. "I don't think I can go to the reception," Right said. Then he turned, without looking at Dumb, and walked out of the crowd, leaving for his hermitage. "And they never saw him again," muttered Lucy. "Oh no!" said Dumb. "A seat at the table will be empty." "He sounded regretful, at least," said Lucy. Dumb watched as Right disappeared around a corner. "Now what?" asked Dumb. "I don't know," Lucy replied. "I guess everything just keeps happening," said Dumb. They walked. "That was a *fine* wedding!" Morton remarked to his wife as they watched Walter and Nicholas leave in the limousine. "It almost makes me wish we had gone through the trouble," Alice said, "when we were that age." "We had a fun time, anyway," said Morton. "But there's something to be said for ceremony," Alice suggested. "It really makes one feel a special part of something." Morton kissed his wife gently, told her that he loved her, and then they walked.

THE RELATIONSHIP

"We are not here."
—William Shakespeare, A *Midsummer Night's Dream*

We have to pray that the road to our town will be built, that they will start the road, and that they will complete the entire road; the road to our town is going to be built, it's going to be finished soon, it's kind of unfolding from the far reaches, slowly; the road is going to be here soon, when it's finished, and then there will be a direct path to our town from everywhere else, and because of that

We are expecting the road to be built, the road that will reach our town from other places that are somewhat distant, or very distant, or really anywhere that is unreachable by our well-maintained system of local streets. We are praying for that road to our town to finally be finished because we want that road, and we need it. We've been waiting for the road to our town. The road is being paved by trustful workers given a good salary, and as they continue to build the road they come closer to finishing it, and every day they work the road is longer, and it's closer to our town. We have put in all the proper requests for the road, we are expecting the road to be built, we

are expecting the road to be finished soon, and we are praying that the road to our town will be built. When the road is
built, when it is finished, when it reaches us from far away,
when that is accomplished, we will be happy, and we'll rejoice
knowing our prayers have been answered, because we knew
what we had to do, we knew that we had to pray; we have to
pray for the road. The road is going to be finished. The road is
going to reach us, finally. And when the road reaches us,

The red lawn mower was old with use; the paint on it was
ugly, and the whole thing was covered with black dust from
the shed, and the wheels had mud and bits of grass caked to
them. The steering wheel was stuck turned left, and the front
wheels stuck turned that way too; the dirty front wheels upset
the fuzzy green rug on the floor of the shed so that the rug was
bunched up in folds under the wheels. Under the worn-out
rug was the dirt of the earth. Rotting lumber was stacked up
on either side of the old lawn mower in the shed, and placed
on one pile of rotting lumber was a pair of thick gloves along
with a rusty hammer, but that was it. No sun came into the
shed, and so little creatures lived there in the darkness, crawling around and eating each other in the absence of light, in
the airless forgotten shed. The old red lawn mower didn't
move, and the lumber didn't move, but the insidious life of
little creatures in the darkness teemed ingloriously all around
the unmoving and useless things in the shed, and the awful
animal writhing didn't stop.

The policeman came to his door. He answered the door.
"Hello, Grover," said the policeman. "Hello," said the man.
"Good afternoon. Please come into my house." His house was
small, and full of rubbish, and the sunlight looked like faded
golden bands in the dirty air. He led the policeman into the

house; the policeman looked around, as if taking it in, as if he had not come to the house before. "You're not taking proper care of yourself," said the policeman, "and that's a shame." The man stopped, and frowned at the policeman, and then said, "Do you want some coffee?" and the policeman said, "Yes, all right," and then he led the policeman into the tiny kitchen. "I like my coffee black," said the policeman.

The tiny kitchen was dark and crowded with soiled dishes. The man cleared a space on the table, and offered the policeman a seat, and then sat across from the policeman. The surface of the kitchen table was made up of sticky grime. He stared at the policeman from across the table without saying anything. The policeman looked at all of his fingernails, and then asked about the coffee. "I'm sorry about the coffee," said the man, and he stood up, and walked to the percolator, and poured coffee into two yellow mugs he found by the sink. "Here," he said, putting the coffee in front of the policeman's face. The policeman took the cup without saying anything and the man sat back down.

The man reached over and pulled a bag of sugar out from under some newspaper on the table, and he poured a lot of sugar into his cup, until the cup overflowed. "Don't do that," said the policeman. "I like the coffee to help me concentrate," the man said. "Have I put you in a situation where it is important to be able to concentrate especially hard?" asked the policeman. The man didn't answer, but he frowned, and he raised his cup to his mouth as if to drink from it. "Did you not hear what I just said?" asked the policeman. "I heard all that you said," the man said. "What was it that I just said, then?" asked the policeman. "You asked me if I need to concentrate because of what you've done," the man said. The policeman hit the table hard with one sudden fist. "That is not what I said. That is not at all what I said! Only a retard with no brains would take what I actually said and misrepresent my words so stupidly. Are you a retard, Grover? I know you're simple. I know you're just a simple man, you've never opened a book in your adult life, you can't do anything right, you're unskilled, you think the road is actually coming (don't you think the road is actually coming?), I know you think the road is actually coming, and you're dull, you're a nobody, and you're a disgrace with nothing to offer, but are you that much of an absolute retard, Grover, that much of a one-hundred-percent retard to have actually misunderstood what I just said in such a blockheaded way? Get that coffee cup away from your mouth! You imbecile! This is why I had to take your wife away. You think these things happen for no reason? Do you think that I'm unfair, or that I'm mean? You don't get it, retard! You don't get anything right, not one simple thing. I try to be nice, but I ask you one question and you can't even do it, Grover, you idiot, you can't even repeat a simple sentence that even a newborn baby could repeat well enough! And that depletes all my patience! Oh you are gross, you are sick. Your brain is full of disease. I want to drain your body of blood. I want to crack your skull open and piss on your retarded little brain. You just don't get it, Grover! I am the hand that takes. I am the hand that takes, retard, I am the hand that takes from you!" said the policeman, rising halfway out of his seat.

The lake had to have a bottom, but it had no bottom. The lake behind the house had to end somewhere, but it didn't. The lake had been said to have edges, because there was that muddy shore, but it wasn't something that kept the same shape, it was something that kept expanding. The lake was definable, but then it wasn't. The lake did not have a bottom to it. The gloomy fabric of the lake was endless. The shiny surface of the lake was a mirror that revealed nothing about the quality of the lake. The muddy shore of the lake was a barrier between the known world apart from the lake and the yawning flux of the lake itself. The lake was absorbing all the meaning around it. When the lake grew, it pulled the meaning of what was around it into its blackness and its depth. When the lake took the meaning into itself it was impossible to tell what happened because there was no seeing deep enough into the lake. There was no way to read the lake. The lake would reflect questions about it without judgment, as if the questions didn't mean anything, and that would raise more questions, but the lake continued to reflect without judgment. The lake had various smells. The lake sounded differently on different days. The muddy shore of the lake was soft. The temperature of the lake was constant, but indescribable. The lake was never stormy. The lake ate the weather. The lake was either an invitation or a warning. The lake was either intelligent or it had no intelligence at all. The lake had to be a problem, but it wasn't. The lake was a birthday party. The lake was a deliberate gesture. The lake was technology. The lake was an animal. The lake that was behind the house. The lake.

"Do you believe in Heaven?" Hamlet asked; he moved his hand across the brown carpet and moved it back. "I don't know," said Francis. The two boys sat on the clean floor of Hamlet's mom's living room. Hamlet looked across to Francis dreamily. "If Heaven existed," Hamlet asked, "what do you think it would be like?" Francis looked as if he was pondering. "I don't know," he said, finally. "It sounds nice." Hamlet leaned toward Francis. "I think if I were going to Heaven I'd want it to be like the beach," he said. "Oh, that does sound nice," said Francis. The walls of the living room were covered with framed family pictures. Francis looked at each one; he saw portraits of Hamlet when he was younger, and of Hamlet's mom and dad when they were still together, and some of the dog. The dog walked through the living room on the way to the kitchen.

Hamlet took Francis' shirt off. "Don't do that," said Francis. Hamlet kissed Francis on the mouth. Hamlet kissed Francis on the mouth again and touched his chest. Francis closed his eyes. Francis took his socks off. "I think my feet are smelly," said Francis. Francis felt the carpet on his bare feet and then on his bare chest. They kissed again. They kissed again. They touched.

"Do you think the road is going to be finished soon?" Hamlet asked. Francis closed his eyes. "I don't know," he said. "Do you think the road is going to be built at all?" asked Hamlet. "I'm not sure," said Francis. "Tell me what you think." The two boys were silent for a long time. "What do you want to be when you grow up?" Hamlet asked. "Um," said Francis, "an astronaut, I guess."

The air was coming out of the air-conditioning unit and it made a low noise constantly. Francis put his shirt on, and held up a book, and held still looking at his own hands holding the book. Hamlet watched what Francis was doing. "What are you doing?" asked Hamlet. Francis listened to the low noise of the air-conditioning unit that was providing cool air. "What are you doing?" asked Hamlet again. "I don't know," said Francis. They kissed again. The dog walked through the living room on the way upstairs. The boys were silent for a long time. Finally, Hamlet spoke. "I guess I don't care if the road is finished or not," he said. "I don't care either, then," said Francis. Hamlet stood up and looked down at Francis. "Do you think we should go out to the field and practice our guns?" he asked. Francis said, "I guess so, if you think it's a good idea." Hamlet got back down on the floor of the living room, and kissed Francis again, and helped Francis put his socks back on.

The air was warm, but there was a breeze. The two boys walked in the tall weeds on the side of the street that led to the field. The trees swayed gently, and the birds both chirped and flew around. "If you could be anybody," asked Hamlet, "who would you be?" Francis was silent for a moment. "That's a hard question," he said, "I'm not sure." Hamlet and Francis held hands as they walked. "Who would you be?" asked Francis. "I asked you first," said Hamlet. "Oh," said Francis, "you're right." Francis looked as if he was pondering. "I would be Cinderella, I guess," he said, finally. "Why would you be Cinderella?" asked Hamlet. "Because she got to be so happy and live in a nice castle," said Francis, "and it was like Heaven." "It's a nice day today," said Hamlet. "It's so nice," said Francis.

The telephone poles leaned in different directions, and cast thin, tall shadows on the pale street that led to the field, and then there weren't telephone poles anymore, and the boys followed along the side of the street, in the tall weeds, and then the street stopped, and there was a twisted metal guard rail, and beyond that the field. "Look, it's a dead dog," said Francis. Hamlet looked around and saw a carcass right where the road ended. "It doesn't look like a dog," said Hamlet. The carcass looked like a matted fur coat, stained with blood and thrown carelessly on the ground. "Maybe it's not a dog anymore," said Francis. Hamlet wiped his foot in the blood on the street, but it was dry. "Do you want to say a prayer?" asked Francis. "No, let's practice our guns like we said," said Hamlet. "Okay," said Francis. Each boy took out his gun, and held it in his hand, then they walked together far into the field.

Each boy aimed at distant trees and shot at them. "Are we

hitting the targets?" asked Francis. "I'm not sure," said Hamlet, "we're too far away." "I think you're probably a good shot," said Francis. "Thanks," said Hamlet. They kept shooting at distant trees, not knowing if they hit them, but after a while started shooting at the ground and the sky. "I'm out of bullets," said Francis. "When we kill everyone," asked Hamlet, "who are you going to kill?" "I don't know," said Francis. "I want to kill the principal and the gym teacher, definitely," said Hamlet. "I would like to kill the gym teacher," said Francis. "All right," said Hamlet, "and then I will kill the basketball team."

The forest was wide; it was dark. That was the forest on the edge of town that was full of tall old pine trees with many needles on every branch that repulsed the sunshine. The forest used to be a farm, a farm that grew pine trees for Christmas, but the farm fell into disrepair, the owner left, and the trees just grew. When the trees were left alone they grew, and more trees came up, and all the trees got so tall, and the branches of each tree reached out in all directions, and thin green needles grew there. All the thin needles of the branches together repulsed the sunshine and cast the forest floor below into darkest shadow. The forest floor was lightless; it was damp. The forest floor was made up of patches of muddy earth and patches of grass, moss, and nettles. The land was uneven. Creatures that loved the darkness lived in the pine tree forest, but they couldn't be seen. The shameful noise of the hidden creatures was heard, and the musty smell of them was detectable, but they lurked in the shadows transparently. The creatures chewed the moss and the slime that grew on the coarse trunks of the pine trees and they swallowed the mushrooms and small flowers that grew out of the muddy earth.

Small and complicated flowers relished the darkness provided by the tall old pine trees and they grew there. When the wind blew, a beastly whistling snarled through the thicket of the branches and many green needles rained furiously down from the branches of the old trees onto the forest floor. When the wind didn't blow, the sound of all the darkness was there in a chorus. The trunk of every tall old pine tree was different; each trunk was covered in different patterns of coarse bark; each trunk was a slightly different color of brown and had a slightly different thickness. There was one trunk of one tall old pine tree that was especially distinct; it was at the center of the pine tree forest. There was one trunk that was marked. One trunk of one pine tree, the pine tree at the center of the forest, had a surface that had been meticulously stripped of coarse bark, and on that tree, on the smooth naked surface of that especially different tree, some words had been carved, with a knife probably. The words had been carved in big, deliberate letters; they read: *On March 15 in the awful year of 1995 the whole world is going to be burned to the ground then all will perish.*

Monday stood in front of the front door of the unfamiliar house that he had been watching, and the door opened, and his son was standing there. "It's you," said Monday. The boy was wet, he was wearing a pink robe, and he was holding a glass quart bottle of milk. "I'm sorry, what?" asked the boy. The man looked at the boy as if expecting something. "I said it's you," said Monday again to his son. "I don't understand," said the boy. The man looked at the boy and began to cry lightly. "Do you need help?" asked the boy. "Is something wrong?" "What's wrong?" asked Monday. "What's wrong?" repeated the boy. "What's wrong with you?" asked Monday. "I'm sorry, what?" asked the boy. "Do you know who I am?"

asked Monday. "Why are you crying? Are you with that—that group?" asked the boy. "Are you here to advertise them?" Monday could not stop his tears. "Come on, darling," he said to the boy, "it's time to go home. It's time to go home. I'm going to take you back, right now, and it will be just like it was." Guardedly, the boy closed the door a little. "I don't understand what you're up to, sir," the boy said, "but I don't appreciate it. If you are looking for a handout, maybe I can spare something. If this is a drug thing, I'm afraid you're going to have to leave before I involve the authorities." Monday tried to stop crying and then he mostly stopped. "Just let me," he said. "I'm okay," he said. "Just listen to me, just stand here and listen to what I'm going to say," he said. The boy looked at Monday, but didn't say anything.

"I've been looking for you," said Monday, "for so long. I don't know what's happened. One day everything was like it always was, but then you weren't there. If you can't recognize me, I don't know what happened. Something terrible has happened, but I don't know what it is. You must remember. If you don't remember, I don't know what's happened, but I'm here now, and you're going to remember. You're my son," Monday said to the boy.

The boy looked at Monday searchingly. "I can't imagine why you're saying this, what you're saying," said the boy. "I just can't possibly divine what you're getting at. What are you doing? What are you doing saying that to me? What do you mean? What do you want?" Monday tried not to cry, he held back his tears, and his face turned red. "What's keeping you here?" asked Monday. "This is my house," said the boy. Monday held his stomach. "Who's inside? Kiddo, look at me, listen to the sound of my voice. Who's inside with you?" asked Monday. He dragged his feet across the welcome mat and looked at his son's face. "I'm not going to put up with this anymore," said the boy, looking cross. "Who's inside the house with you?" Monday asked again. "Nobody's inside my house with me!" said the boy. "Nobody's inside my house with me! I've been patient enough with you. You just go now or I'm going to call someone." Tears came out of Monday's eyes and went down his red face. Monday looked at his son, saw his son was closing the door, and he gnashed his teeth, and as he watched the face of his son as the door began to close, he cried and he moaned, and then he burst forward, without another word he leapt at his son, and fell on him, and the boy dropped the glass quart bottle of milk he was holding, and the boy went down, and hit the floor, and Monday landed on top of him. The boy screamed and Monday closed the door to the house with a kick. The entryway to the house was clean and empty; the wooden floor was shiny. The bottle the boy was holding rolled away; the spilt milk formed a puddle and then trickled down in between the slats of the wood of the floor.

Monday was on top of his son, keeping him on the shiny wooden floor, pressing his elbows into the boy's chest, and stroking the boy's wet face desperately with his hands. "No!" cried the boy. "What are you doing? Stop! Get off!" "My son," said Monday; his tears landed on the boy's eyelids. The boy struggled. "Are you serious?" asked the boy. "I knew I'd find you," said Monday, "now things are going to be good again." "There's little of value here. I live alone, I'm a widower, I don't keep nice things. There's the radio, and the television, and the computers, but that's it. Everything else just has sentimental value. Take what you have to, but don't hurt me. There's no reason to hurt me!" said the boy. "My son, my son," Monday said again and again. "You have to be crazy! You must be off some medication. I can help you. I won't call the police. Let me go, I'll help you understand the mistake you're making," said the boy. Monday touched his son's face and he touched his son's wet hair. "My son," he said again. "I'm not your son," said the boy. "What's your name?" "Your father, Monday," said Monday. "Monday," said the boy, "I'm not your son. Did you hear that? It's absurd. Monday, I'm not your son, I'm a full-grown man. I'm a thirty-three-year-old man, Monday, I'm not a child, I'm a computer programmer, I'm a widower who lives alone, no children, no children in this house at all."

Monday picked up his son and carried the boy into the living room of the unfamiliar house. The boy, so much smaller than Monday, could not resist. Monday put the boy down on a pretty white couch with floral decoration and sat on top of him. The living room was full of light, and white furniture, but nothing else except a magazine on the floor. "If you let me go upstairs, I can show you my identification," said the boy, "and you'll see who I am, that I'm not who you think I am. There's no way I can be." "This house is so empty," said Monday. "Some things I couldn't be with," said the boy, "when my wife died. She died of AIDS. Some of her things I gave to her sisters." "What's happened to you?" asked the man. The sunshine came through the windows and made squares of light on the pale carpet. Monday looked around, and he saw a table with nothing on it, and a mirror. Monday saw a place on the pale carpet where little indents showed that some other piece of furniture had been there for a long time, but had been taken away. "I don't know what's happened," said Monday, "but you're a boy, I can see that you're a child, and I know that you're my son, my twelve-year-old son." "That's not right," said the boy. "You have to realize that what you think you see is a problem. Your delusions are causing a giant problem right now." "It's time to stop playing pretend," said Monday.

"I don't know what happened, but you're not in a dream, and this is not a game of pretend," he said. "This is real life, this is what's happening right now, and you're here, you, my son, whoever you think you are, or are saying you are because I don't know why, you're not that person, you are my twelve-year-old son, my boy," he said. Monday stroked the boy's face and he smiled. His son couldn't respond. The boy was still with panic. "Your face," said Monday. He sighed. "I'm so happy right now," he said. He looked at the boy, he looked at his son's eyes, and he saw there was no expression in them anymore, as if the boy had retreated into himself, put everything about himself somewhere else. Monday did this, saw this, and was silently thoughtful. Finally, he spoke, and his son shook and quickly looked at him when he spoke. "It will all be better soon," Monday said. "I'm going to have to do something bad now, but when you're better you'll understand." His son opened his mouth as if to speak. Monday closed his fist and hit the boy's face. His son made an injured sound. Monday hit his son's face again, hard, and again, before the boy could make an injured sound again. Monday hit his son's face again, and then the boy didn't make a sound and didn't move at all. Monday released a deep breath, and stood up from where he was sitting on top of his son, and stood over the boy, and looked at the unmoving boy for a long time. Then Monday picked up his son's body and carried him away in his arms. Without looking again at the house, he carried his son out into the yard, and then put him in the car. He placed his son delicately in the passenger seat, and then walked around to the other side, and sat behind the wheel of the car, and sat there, and looked out of the windshield. "Everything's right again," said Monday. "When you wake up you'll be away from here. And everything that has happened to you, you'll be away from. You'll be with me. It will be like it was between us. And I'll make sure this never happens again. I swear on my life I will never, ever let anything bad happen to you again for the rest of your life! I'll take you away from here. We'll go somewhere we can be safe. They're going to build the road. When it's finished, we'll drive away. And we'll keep driving. And we'll never come back," he said, and he started the car.

The earth is moving. We have to pray for the road to reach us. We want the road to come and the road is going to come. When the road is finished, our prayers will be answered. We expect the road. The road is going to be built. There is every reason for the road. We're waiting; the road is coming. The road will be built because of our efforts. There is no way to stop the road. We want the road; we anticipate that the road is going to be built. The road, when it appears, will be a blessing. We will have the road we want. There is no doubt the road will come. The road is going to reach us; the road is going to change everything. And when the road is done, when it reaches us,

The road is here now. And when the road comes

GAME BELLY

A room like this: a fluffy chair, white and napping; a burdened shelf of yellow books; the splintered wood of a knowing floor; a decorative illustration of a simply drawn rabbit, framed and hung above a low green table upon which flowers stand in a quiet vase, dying; a square of lamps, baldly bright; a frowning plastic telephone mounted on the wall by the only door: this is what I find when I enter, what I create for myself when I read these particular objects as I walk into the sunless space and feel myself contained again—but lately I do not find him there. And the game belly is missing.

The sky is a lighted black; clouds crawl along between the tall buildings, seeming like other things. The stairs leading down into the discotheque are in the middle of the block, between a bodega protected in the night by a metal lattice and an empty, yellow laundromat. The street looks wet, but isn't; it makes a sound like the ocean when occasional taxicabs drive by, none of them stopping. A man with broad shoulders is standing in front of the stairs leading down into the discotheque. He is sturdy but has a small head and wrinkled face—fiercely white circles of eyes are set deep in the wrinkled face. He watches each taxicab drive quickly by, starts of blunt yellow, and he watches the leaning fence beyond the street, on the other side, where there is nothing but dirt, and litter, and strands of weeds. He can smell the river nearby. In his left ear he has placed a plastic earpiece that is connected wirelessly to the mobile phone in his right pants pocket. His blockish right hand is in his right pants pocket, tenderly stroking the phone. There is a voice in his ear, coming from the earpiece, transmitted to the earpiece from the phone. He says nothing but the voice speaks; it's a woman's voice. She says, "Bob, oh! Bob, I'm so hard for you. My dick is so stiff and eager. I can tell you're all wet; your pussy is melting for me. I'm stroking your cunt gently with my fingers. Do you like that, Bob? I know you do. I know your cunt is hungry for me. I'm stroking it, Bob, oh yes, yes—it feels so good. It's so soft! I just put a finger inside. Ooh, you like that, don't you, Bob? Yeah. I'll be as gentle as you want. Here comes another inside. Yeah, just like that. I know you love the way I feel pressed up against you like this, putting myself inside of you. Oh! Oh, Bob. I'm going to start stroking faster. Are you ready for this? I know you are. You don't even have to say it. I like the silent type."

A boy and a girl climb up the stairs—the boy, grimacing but careful, supporting the delicate girl who is slumped up against him. The boy leans on the railing of the stairs, he pulls the two of them forward, step by step, with his right hand and arm, while holding the girl upright with his left hand and arm. His arms tremble from the strain. The girl has wilted; her head curls into his neck, her eyes flutter, her lips press together in soundless motions. Her legs, nearly graceful with unease, bend forward with every step the boy makes. The boy groans and then he says, "Come on." The boy has black hair and a pale face; he begins to sweat on the sixth step, midway up the stairs to the street. The girl has red hair that is tied fancifully in several buns and she has a pale face.

The discotheque is almost closed and the bar is sparsely attended except for two laughing women and a kid with long hair, wearing a tattered suit, who is alone. The laughing women drink shots of whiskey, and then stand up, and escort one another away from the bar to dance. The kid with long hair looks into the mirror that is mounted, stretching, over the bar. He sees the reflection of a burly man and a skinny woman who sit close together on a couch by the bathroom, kissing. The woman slips her left leg in between the legs of the man, and their faces touch, and they kiss. The man has his left arm wrapped around the woman, his right hand pressed against her left leg right below her buttocks. The woman has her hands wrapped around the man's waist. Two drinks sit on a table next to them. As the kid with long hair watches, before he gets tired of watching, he sits slouched, touching the glass in front of him compulsively, and then he gets tired of watching. The glass is filled with melting ice cubes but is empty. It sits on a napkin that is so wet it is almost translucent. The napkin carries the soggy imprint of the round bottom of the glass. The bartender is a short black girl. She walks to the edge of the bar and pushes a button on the stereo system; a new song begins to play. The girl walks disinterestedly up and down the bar, from the furthest edge where the stereo system is set up to near where the kid with long hair sits alone. The kid begins to follow the path of the bartender. She looks angelic in the dim light, walking past the rows of bottles of liquor and wine. There is a black light turned on and glowing just above the cash register and when the girl passes before it her head is silhouetted by a neon glow and looks as if it is surrounded by a heavenly nimbus. When she passes by the watching kid, he makes a decision. He raises his glass and requests another drink. When he raises his glass, the wet napkin sticks and rises with it. The bartender notices this and smiles. "Same?" she says to him. "Please," the boy yells, trying to be heard over the music, but so loud he sounds as if he's screaming. The bartender frowns at that, but she takes a new glass from underneath the bar, puts ice in it, and then some jiggers of gin, and then pours in tonic water from a bottle until the glass is full. Lightly, the glass is shiny; the glass is the most luminous thing at the bar. The bartender lifts the glass, careful not to let the drink spill over, and places it in front of the kid with long hair. "Thank you," the kid says, quietly. He looks into the bartender's eyes and reaches with his right hand into his right back pants pocket for his wallet. The bartender closes her eyes and shrugs. "Last call," she says. "On the house." "Oh," the kid says, "oh, thank you." He doesn't consider plucking out a dollar tip for her anyway, but the bartender doesn't react to this discourtesy; instead she leans on the bar, and sighs exaggeratedly, and says, "Almost out of here." The kid with long hair brings his glass to his lips. "I've never seen you before," the bartender says. The bartender and the kid are looking at each other, but nothing is happening. "Is that good or bad?" asks the kid. "Fine," says the bartender, "I don't know." "I'm new in town," says the kid, "is why." "Oh—where'd you come from?" asks the bartender. "White Dog," the kid says. "Pretty far," the bartender nods. The kid is silent, but then finally he admits, "I want to be a writer." "I see," says the bartender, "you're one of *those*. My ex-boyfriend thought he was a writer for a while. He was an asshole. Anyway, for any one of you guys you're in the right place." The kid asks, "This bar?" The bartender laughs. "Maybe," she says. "It's a good place." The kid is silent, but then finally he says, "Listen—what are you doing after this?" "Oh," says the bartender, "after I close?" "After you close the bar, yeah," the kid says. The bartender pushes herself away from the bar and stares at the ceiling thoughtfully, briefly. "Um," she says, "definitely going home and going to sleep. Why?" The kid with long hair laughs nervously. "I guess it is late," he says. "How old are you?" the bartender asks. "Oh, uh, twenty," says the kid. "I guess you have a fake," says the bartender. "Oh, yeah," the kid admits. "Your secret's safe with me," the bartender says. "Thanks," says the kid. "So—" "So, yeah, as I was saying," the bartender interrupts him, "It's late. Maybe not for a young bohemian artist type like you, but for a simple gal like me who has places to be in the morning; I need my beauty rest," the bartender says. "I just thought," says the kid, "I don't know what I thought." "Well, enjoy your drink," says the bartender. "Nice talking to you." She walks away from him, to the cash register, where she opens the drawer and begins to count the money inside. The kid looks at her back for a long time. He picks up his cocktail and drinks it.

The kid with long hair, wearing a tattered suit, climbs slowly up the stairs. He counts each step and finds there are twelve. The night air is dry, but wet seeming. The temperature is perfectly cold for the night: just slightly colder than what is comfortable. Frowning, the kid stands on the sidewalk. He looks at the watch on his left wrist and then he looks at the leaning fence beyond the street, on the other side, where this is nothing but dirt, and litter, and strands of weeds. He can smell the river nearby. Things are black but nothing is, in earnest, dark. He is standing in what is only the city's darkness—glowing darkness. He is standing next to, barely noticing, a man with broad shoulders who is placed in front of the entrance to the discotheque. The man is standing still, right hand in his pocket, concentrating. Standing on the other side of the kid with long hair, closer to the crumbling façade of the building, near a Siamese fire hydrant, is a boy with black hair and a pale face; he is watching a girl with a pale face and red hair that is tied fancifully in several buns; she is tucked into herself, sitting on the ground and leaning against the wall. The boy and the girl are smoking cigarettes. The girl's cigarette is brown and sweet smelling and the boy's cigarette is hand-rolled. The kid with long hair can hear that they are talking and what they are saying. "I can speak fine now," says the girl. "Fine," says the boy. "I'm not that drunk," says the girl. "I'd like to see you stand," says the boy. "I'd like to see you not be a dick, for once," says the girl. "I'm sorry," says the boy. "You always say, 'I'm sorry,'" says the girl, "but mean it for once." "I'm sorry," says the boy. "You said it exactly the same as before!" says the girl. "I'm sorry," says the boy. "What am I going to do about you?" asks the girl. "Drown me in the river," says the boy. "I deserve it." "I thought you had listened to me when we were talking about how you have to stop behaving that way and stop bringing up certain things all the time," says the girl. "What was I bringing up?" says the boy. "What we're not talking about!" says the girl. The kid watches them talk, but then the girl sees him watching and yells, "What are you looking at? Do I look like a famous actress or something?" "Uh . . ." the kid says. He turns around and watches the taxicabs driving by. He walks closer to the curb and sticks his right hand high in the air, awkwardly. No taxicabs stop for him. He lowers his hand, embarrassed, and scratches his head. The girl begins to laugh. The broad-shouldered man placed in front of the entrance to the discotheque suddenly says, "Okay, baby, goodbye—see you soon," seemingly as if to no one, or to the air. The kid studies the taxicabs as they pass, starts of blunt yellow, and then decides to try to hail one again. He leans further into the street and sticks his right hand high in the air, purposefully. "The cabs aren't stopping," the sitting girl finally yells at the kid with long hair. The kid looks at the girl and the boy; the girl begins to laugh again. The boy calmly rolls a cigarette and offers it to the kid. The kid walks toward the boy and plucks the cigarette out of his hand. The boy then offers the kid matches. The girl is still laughing. "Cabs!" she says in between her laughter. The kid lights his cigarette and then returns the matches; he inhales the smoke and coughs violently. Then he turns around and walks away. The kid walks in an unknown direction, framed by the mostly sleeping buildings, looking down at the bruised concrete. The girl and the boy remain as they are. "Jesus," says the girl. "Stop laughing," says the boy. "What a retard," says the girl. "You should be nicer to people," says the boy. "Who are you to say?" says the girl. "You're right," says the boy. The broad-shouldered man, who has been standing still in his place, approaches the boy where he stands. "Can you roll me a spliff with this?" he asks, pulling a plastic bag filled with marihuana out of his left pants pocket. "Yes," says the boy. "Jesus," says the girl, but she doesn't move. The boy produces his pouch of tobacco again, and carefully rolls a cigarette with a mixture of tobacco and marihuana, and then hands it to the man with the pack of matches. "Thank you," says the man. He lights the marihuana cigarette. "No problem," says the boy. After he takes a drag, the man silently offers the cigarette to the boy, but the boy shrugs. The man nods, hands back the matches, and walks toward the subway. "We're going to be here forever," the girl says. She gnashes her teeth. She pulls her mobile phone out of her pocket and checks the time. "Not much longer," says the boy. "Sit down next to me," the girl tells the boy. The boy looks at her, and takes a drag off his dying cigarette, and tosses it into the wet seeming street, and, moving his waist, not his legs, looks around him, and sees the leaning fence beyond the street, on the other side, where there is nothing there but dirt, and litter, and strands of weeds, and then he decides to sit down. He does not look at the girl, but pulls his pouch of tobacco out of his left pants pocket and begins to roll another cigarette. "Stop chain smoking," says the girl. The girl is smoking a cigarette that is brown, and sweet smelling, and almost finished. "Come closer to me," she says, like a baby. "You're sick drunk," the boy says, looking at the cigarette he is rolling. "Am not," says the girl. "You're going to throw up," says the boy, "any minute." "No I'm *not*, Justin!" the girl says. The boy looks up at the sky, sees if he can finish rolling his cigarette without looking at it. The sky is a lighted black; what city brightness there is reflects off the crawling clouds. The boy says nothing. "I want to be close to you," says the girl. The boy says nothing.

The streetlamps' weeping dull light reflects off the windshield of a serious black town car, driving. The driver, dressed in a white shirt and black slacks, stops the car in front of the discotheque that is in the middle of the block. Taxicabs drive by unstoppably. The driver presses a plastic button, and the passenger-side window lowers, and he can see a boy and a girl sitting next to each other, next to a Siamese fire hydrant and also the crumbling façade of the building.

The boy helps the girl with a pale face and folding limbs into the backseat of the chauffeured town car, and then he walks around to the other side, and enters the backseat through the opposite door. He looks weary. "Fuck you," the girl tells the boy. "What?" the boy says. "We're going to 25 Branch Street, please—across the bridge," the girl tells the driver. "Yes ma'am," the driver says. The driver taps a few times on a computer screen that is attached to the dashboard, then he drives. "Why 'fuck you'?" asks the boy. "No," says the girl, "fuck *you*." "I know," says the boy. The girl leans wickedly toward him, making the boy sigh lightly, implacably. The girl rests her head on his shoulder. "You're drunk," says the girl, "really drunk." "I know," says the boy. The girl brushes her lips across the side of the boy's neck; he sighs again and whispers. The girl says, "You're ill. You have alcoholism." "Maybe," the boy says. "From your mother," the girl says. "I'm not glad you can talk now," says the boy. "Sometimes I feel like our conversations occur in a vacuum," she says, "or on a vacation." "Don't get like this," he says. "*You* get to say whatever you want when you're drunk," says the girl. "You talk and talk." The boy says nothing.

Here in this room it could be night; it is. I'm in this lightless room, turning on the square of lamps, baldly bright. When I sit down in the fluffy chair it wakes up and says hello. The flowers are all dead. He hasn't returned. The game belly is missing. It's been me here with my abandonment, my worry, my loneliness, my pathetic fallacy, and my narration—since everything changed. I remember when he showed me the girl with a pale face and red hair that she ties fancifully in several buns; I know how long ago that was because I always count my time. I looked at her from across the table and thought, *Now what kind of girl is that?* Maybe I don't know why people do what they do, but I can see it. I sit in the fluffy chair, with a browning book in my lap, and I read one sentence, then I read another sentence, and then I read a word, and another word, and another, and I count my time. I look up from the book. I watch the frowning plastic telephone mounted on the wall by the door as if I'm waiting for it to say something. There is a hole shaped like the game belly in me somewhere. The absence gnaws at me just like the betrayal. Maybe that's not as bad as how and what I know about the lighted blackness of night outside this room, but maybe it's worse. That glow. The telephone is simply silent, frowning and unresponsive. I stand up, walk to it, and pick it up to make it speak, but can only hear something that sounds busy and empty. I hang up the phone, and turn off the square of lamps, and sit down in the vacuity of the lightless room, on the fluffy chair, and pick up my book, and read one sentence, then another sentence, and then a word, and another word, and another, as if I can see the page or as if it matters. Soon I'm going to go outside.

The backseat of the chauffeured town car is contained—there is an unremembered cushiony darkness. The boy and the girl sit together, in the backseat, close to one another, touching each other. The city looks fast, and tall, and careless from the windows. "Oh," says the girl to the boy, "happy birthday." The boy says, "I hate tomorrows." The girl is resting her pale face on the boy's chest; her hands are wrapped, tucked into his right shoulder. The boy has a tentative arm across their intertwined legs; his fingers press her bare knee. "I'm a terrible person," says the boy. The boy looks at the puffy leather headrest of the driver's seat; he hears the street like the ocean. "You are," says the girl, "coming to my house." The boy says, "Yes." "You'll do something *terrible* to me," says the girl. "Probably," says the boy. There is a silence between them—the ocean—somewhere there could be birds but there aren't; and the driver coughs. The driver makes a right turn and he sees the bridge ahead. "You like me," says the girl. "Yes," the boy says. Her face touches his face, and both move until their lips touch, and then they are kissing. They aren't kissing anymore. The boy looks at the puffy headrest of the driver's seat, sees its leather shine like an insect's eye. The driver casts glances at the girl from his mirror. "Excuse me," he says politely, "I don't want to be rude—I'm not supposed to make conversation with the passengers—but can I ask you a question, ma'am?" The girl sits upright a little; the boy doesn't move. "You're more than welcome to," says the girl. "Are you an actress?" asks the driver. The girl smiles slightly. "Yes," she says, "that's my profession." "I knew it," says the driver. "You were in that film about the crazy painter, right?" "I was," she says. "You played his mistress," the driver says. "His muse," says the girl. "I took my girlfriend to see that movie," the driver says, still looking at her in his mirror, and then the road briefly, and then her. "I hope you both enjoyed it," says the girl. "Why do you do this?" asks the boy, kissing the girl's ear suddenly. "Yeah," says the driver, "I'm going to have to tell her I saw you." "Say I say hello," says the girl. "I will," says the driver. The driver drives the car across the bridge that is suspended over the river.

The girl looks out the window, briefly, but nothing happens. The car is moving forward; the boy says nothing. The girl finally leans forward a little and asks the driver, "Is it okay if I smoke in here?" The driver politely shrugs and, looking at her in his mirror, says, "That's fine between us, ma'am." "Courtesy," says the girl to the boy. She falls back onto the seat and searches her purse for her pack of cigarettes. "We smoke a lot of cigarettes," she says. Her cigarettes are brown and sweet smelling. As she lights one, the boy takes out his pouch of tobacco and begins to roll one of his own for himself. "Tonight is fun—was," says the girl. The boy says nothing, produces a finely rolled cigarette. He takes out his matches, and strikes one, and lights his cigarette with it, then offers the lit match to the girl, who uses it too. "Funny . . . tonight was fun, right?" asks the girl. "You drank too much and you spent too much money on drinks," says the boy. Cigarette smoke is curling around both of them, so the boy presses a button that opens the window next to him, then he ashes his cigarette out of the window. "But it was *fun*—you had fun, you know," says the girl. The boy says, "I don't enjoy your friends." "They're our friends, both of ours," says the girl, "and you enjoy Aaron." "No, he was just talking to me all night about nothing," the boy says. The girl says, "He was talking about something! You had fun." "They're all vapid," the boy says. The girl says, "Fuck you." She clucks lightly and withdraws her mobile phone from her purse. She presses buttons rapidly on her phone, balancing her cigarette between two slender fingers, sending a message to a mobile phone elsewhere. "You try to be an elitist, but it's just embarrassing," she says. "If you stopped trying to alienate everyone to feel above them and admitted that we're all of us serious artists, it wouldn't be so painful for me to take you out like this, with them, for us." "Maybe it's for the best," the boy says. Then the boy says nothing and the girl is quiet. The boy looks out the window, but does not react to what he sees there. The girl's face glows weakly blue in the light of her phone, which she handles. She types tiny letters into her phone one at a time, sending out electronic messages. "I'm talking to Aaron right now," she says. "He says he enjoys *you*." She types and says, "He says he's dating that model girl from Alaska, but I just don't know why he doesn't come out and admit he's a homo. Don't you think?" "I don't remember him saying anything interesting," says the boy, "and I don't care if he's queer." "I know he slept with what's-his-face once—the pseudocolumnist," she tells him. "I have a weight," says the boy. "It's tremendous." The girl hands him what is left of her cigarette. "Throw that out the window?" she says. The boy turns away from her, and tosses the cigarette out the window, along with his, and then pushes the button, and the window rolls up again. "Get closer to me again," says the girl. "Yes," says the boy. "Aaron says he's going to bed," she says, looking at her phone still. The boy says, "Okay."

The broad-shouldered man travels miles underground, under the river, through the exasperated stink of the contained tunnel air, to arrive in the neighborhood where he lives. When he walks up the steps from the subway, I can see him in the flickering glow of an all-night bodega's yellow storefront. The door to the bodega is locked, but there is a thick, stained plastic box installed in the front window, mounted to turn in circles, through which somebody can place his order and place money in the box, so that the tired man working inside can turn the box, pick up the money, and give the person on the street his purchase with the box again. There is a line in front of the box of anxious men all buying malt liquor at this hour. The broad-shouldered man glances at the line, but walks on. He walks in my direction. I am standing in front of a tall, horrible building, the entrance of which is made out of stainless steel and foggy bulletproof glass. The man looks at me but is about to walk by. "Excuse me, sir," I say. He is tentative, but slows down. "Can I talk to you for a minute?" I ask. "You shouldn't be out here this late, talking to strangers," he says. "I know," I say, "but it's important." "Where do you live?" he asks. "You should go home." "I'm okay," I say, "but—I just need your help for a second, I need you to tell me if you've seen something I can't find." He notices I have a piece of paper in my hand. I hold the piece of paper up for him to see; I've drawn a picture of the game belly on it. "I'm missing this," I say. "What is it?" he asks, looking. "It's very important," I say. He takes the piece of paper from my hand and brings it closer to his face—to his fiercely white circles of eyes. "This," he says, "looks familiar—but I don't know why." "Have you seen it?" I ask. "I'm not sure," he says. "I don't think so." "Try and remember," I say. "I'm sorry," he says. "I just don't know. I can't tell for sure." "Well thank you anyway, I guess," I say, waiting for the paper to be returned. "Thanks for your time." The man continues to look at the drawing. "I'm very sorry," he says. "I lost something once too." "What was that?" I ask. "I lost my old girl, Beatrice," he says, lowering the paper. "They took her and did all sorts of shit to her . . . beat her, and raped her, and cut her, and fucked her up the ass." "Oh. Oh, no," I say. "Yeah—I went around with her picture after she disappeared, went around the neighborhood in my friend's car and stopped everyone walking by, showed them the picture and asked if they had seen her go away with anyone, or seen her at all. I never found her after that," he says. "That's the most awful thing I've heard," I say. "I'm sorry." He says, "No, it's so long ago now . . . you just got me thinking. I shouldn't have brought it up. Listen, I hope you find what you're looking for here," he hands me the piece of paper back, "but you can't be standing out like this, this late at night, stopping people. You'll go missing next. Be careful." I say, "Yes." He turns away and walks into the building.

The broad-shouldered man walks up dozens of dirty linoleum stairs to stand in front of a green door. When he stands on the mangy welcome mat in front of the green door, he sticks his right hand into his right pants pocket and digs around his phone to find a set of keys. Using the keys, stuck in his block-ish fist, he unlocks the door and steps inside. The lights are on and somebody is waiting. The man takes off his baseball cap and coat, and places them on the floor next to a row of shoes, and then removes the earpiece from his ear, and puts it in his pocket with his phone. "Mercy?" he says, calling down the entryway. "Kids okay tonight?" He walks forward and finds a stout woman in the kitchen, sitting and watching a portable television set that she keeps on the plastic dining table. She stops watching the show, and looks at the man, and says, "Yes, Bob—I fed them ice cream for dessert, and checked their math problems, and put them down." The man and the woman find each other in the middle of the kitchen, embrac-ing. "Okay at work?" she asks. "Not without your help," he says into her hair. They stand this way for a while. "I'm going to turn the show off," says the woman finally. He follows her out of the kitchen and into the bedroom. One of the walls in the bedroom looks burnt. The sheets on the bed are old, but clean. The man sits down on the bed and takes off his shoes, from the right foot and then the left, and then takes off his socks, right and left. The woman sings a song. "I like that," says the man when the woman is done. The man takes off his shirt, and walks to his dresser, and puts on another shirt. He stands in front of the bed, and takes off his pants, and picks up his pants, removes the contents of both pockets, puts ev-erything he has removed on top of the dresser, and then folds up the pants, and puts them on top of the dresser too. Then he sits back down on the bed. The woman sits down on the bed next to him. "Security in the morning?" asks the woman. "Nope," says the man, "but driving." "Oh," she says. "Want to take a shower?" asks the man. "Already did," says the woman.

"I'm going to," he says. "I'll see you back here," she says. "It's late; I'm getting in bed." The man stands up, rubs his feet into the coarse carpet, and turns to look at the sitting woman. "Mercy," he says, "do you really like to call me at work?" The woman looks at him without a change in her expression. She says, "I don't mind it, Bob." And then the man leaves the room.

The boy with black hair and a pale face looks at the puffy leather headrest of the driver's seat of the chauffeured town car, across the bridge. "I'm complicated," he says. "You're an asshole," says the girl he is sitting with, touching. "I'm destructive," says the boy. "You're a solipsist," says the girl. "You're right," says the boy. "It's silly," says the girl. "We're drunk." The boy says, "You're sick drunk." "Am not," says the girl. The boy turns to the girl, briefly. "Am I hurting you enough?" he asks. "I am wondering." "Fuck you," she replies. The boy says nothing. "We're drunk," the girl says again. The boy says, "Don't make me angry! 'We're drunk. We're *drunk*.' I'm angry. I'm terrible. 'We're drunk.' That doesn't change anything. That doesn't change—" "Don't say it!" says the girl. "What was I going to say?" asks the boy. "Don't fucking say what you were going to say!" says the girl. "But what was I going to say?" asks the boy. "Don't *say* what you were *going* to!" says the girl. The boy says nothing for some time. "Say you're sorry," says the girl. "I'm sorry," says the boy. "Oh fuck you!" the girl cries. The boy looks at the puffy leather headrest of the driver's seat of the chauffeured town car. Most of the buildings on the other side of the river are low and long; the sky is lower; the streets are higher to the sky.

The car turns left and right through the half-darkness of the city's night. In the backseat, the boy and the girl are kissing. They kiss, and touch, and are close to one another, and communicate, as they kiss, only in sighs and whispered sighs. "Almost there," the girl finally says. Her lips brush lightly against his lips when she speaks. He inhales her breath. She closes her eyes. He opens his eyes. There is silence between them. Then the boy says, into her mouth, "Game belly." Everything stops; the car keeps moving. The girl opens her eyes, and at first says nothing, but makes inchoate noises of displeasure in her throat. She backs away from him slightly. The boy and the girl are looking at each other directly—the girl looks awestruck; the boy looks emotionless. There is silence between them. Finally the boy asks, "What are you going to say?" "I don't know," says the girl. "I don't think I'm really talking right now." The street sounds like the ocean. "Stop the car, please, driver—pull over," the girl says. The driver does, and when the car is stopped, the girl slides fully away from the boy, reaches for the handle to the door to the backseat, and opens the door with a precise gesture, looking at the boy. Then she turns around and pokes her head out of the slightly open door and vomits onto the street. The girl's vomit, thickly splattering, comes out of her mouth and onto the street and onto the rear wheel of the car. When she finishes, she pulls her head back inside, and closes the door, and with her right hand wipes her mouth like an impossible bird. The boy says nothing. "Are you okay, ma'am?" asks the driver. The girl doesn't answer the question. "Is there a problem?" asks the driver. "She's just sick drunk," says the boy. "Keep driving." The driver follows the instruction; the car begins again to move. The boy leans toward the girl. "Almost there," he says into her ear.

The kid with long hair, wearing a tattered suit, walks alone in the unfamiliar city, without direction. He looks lonely and senseless in the glowing blackness. The city is tall, and old, and hungry looking. The kid keeps both his hands in his pants pockets and walks rigidly, step by step, with empty determination. There is nobody around to give him directions home. Everywhere he goes he sees ghostly emptiness; the city is a guilty, evacuated thing. The boy is slightly drunk—his face is warm and scrunched. He sits on a park bench that is thick with layered paint. There is nothing for him on the bench. Standing up, he crosses the street, and crosses back, and walks several blocks in the direction he came from. He sees that some windows are dark but some windows are left lit. He walks, and turns a corner, and sees a tiny statue on a concrete island in the middle of the street. There are no cars, so he walks onto the street, and walks onto the concrete island, and admires the statue up close. It is a statue of a young girl, leaning forward slightly, holding a basket in her left hand. The kid with long hair removes his right hand from his pants pocket, and reaches out, and touches the girl. She looks something like the bartender at the discotheque, but with a sad expression. She just stands there in place. The kid with long hair just stands there, and looks at her, touching her, and then he wrings his hands. The night doesn't change around them. Finally he says, "I'm going home," and again walks in the direction he came from.

The kid with long hair walks in the middle of the street now; he walks fast and when he walks fast enough the street almost sounds like the ocean again—but there are no cars, or any living person except him anywhere around where he is. "Nobody can hear me," he says. "What am I doing here? I mean, here? Maybe I like being where nobody can hear. I'm cold."

He doesn't say anything else, continues to walk, and walks. He can't tell if he is walking toward the river or away from it; he does not pass a map, or a subway station, or bus stop, or anything that could provide him either with context or the opportunity of transportation somewhere else. What happens in the night is that things retreat; what is left is the battered part of the city, growling yet reposed in its lighted darkness, sour glow. The streetlamps shine down upon the vacancy with irony. They shine down weak, insincere electric light, and one of them in particular shines light that reflects off of a glimmering object behind the glass of a dark storefront and, because of that, down an obscure alley between two reaching buildings, and off of the surface of the destroyed remains of the game belly. When the kid with long hair finds the shine, he stops walking as fast, and then he stops walking. He sees the light from the particular streetlamp reflecting off of something down the alley, and he watches it for a while. He turns to see how the light is operating—that it is first reflecting off of a glimmering object behind the glass of a dark storefront, and therefore finding what he sees lit in the alley, and he smiles from knowing. Then he decides to walk toward what he sees. From the street, he walks onto the sidewalk, and from the sidewalk he slips carefully into the alley, walking slowly, with reserved steps, toward the mysterious object. His body blocks the light for a moment and the object stops shining, but he bends over to allow the reflection to find it again, so he can see where it is to approach it. The alley smells like hopeless garbage; rats live there, feasting on what's thrown out. The kid steps on broken glass and on torn copies of last month's newspapers as he is surrounded by the desperate smell. The place has a feeling of a place where danger happens; refuse and things that don't belong to or happen in the light are there. The kid keeps walking toward the shiny thing. It's torn apart on the ground where the alley ends. He stands above it, but then he kneels down closer. It's the game belly, but not what the game belly used to be—what it is now. The kid looks at it for a long time as the light lights up his face; it's the light reflected from the shattered parts of the ruined thing. The kid holds his hair out of his face and thinks about what he sees. He looks as if he understands what it was before: a thing of beauty. He holds his hair with his left hand and with his right hand he covers his mouth. The kid, kneeling there, begins to cry. He stares at the game belly: its perfection destroyed with violence and discarded—the lost game belly. The kid with long hair kneels, crying quietly, as if time doesn't matter because of this atrocity. When he stands, he looks away from the sight, and does not turn around again to take a final look or to pick it up and bring it with him, but he walks away as simply as that, touching the wall of the alley with his left hand to keep his balance in the darkness. He finds the sidewalk again, and then he finds the street, and turns and begins to walk in the direction he came from. Down the middle of the street he walks, wiping his tears on the sleeves of his tattered suit, before he begins to run, not crying any longer. He starts to run as fast as he can, and begins to smile because the street sounds like the ocean again. Then a car strikes him. He rolls over the yellow hood of the taxicab and off of the side, hitting the street and seeing the car drive away without stopping. He says something about it, but the words aren't real. Once more the street is quiet and empty, except now for the kid's body in the middle of the intersection. As if he doesn't understand what just happened, he starts to smile a bloody smile. He tries to stand up, but something is wrong and he can't manage to. He can't quite move properly, as if he's not awake, but trying to move his sleeping limbs anyway. If he was able to turn his head to see his chest he would see the accident, but he can't. He doesn't get up—he just becomes pale, looking unusually cold even for the night weather in autumn, and he barely moves at all.

In the backseat of a chauffeured town car, the boy with black hair and a pale face sits apart from the girl with a pale face and red hair that is tied fancifully in several buns. The backseat of the car is contained—there is an unremembered cushiony darkness. That's what's between them, and everything else. The girl is breathing heavily; her clenched fists are white like the meat of a tooth. "I don't think we understand how much of a badness is in me," the boy says, finally. "I'm not going to cry or anything," says the girl, but she doesn't look as if she understands what she says. The boy says, "Thank you." "It doesn't matter," says the girl. "I'm sorry," says the boy. The girl says, "All right." The boy says nothing. The girl says, "You have to promise, really promise, never to talk about certain things again. What I did, or what you did, or whatever it is that happened, doesn't matter, because you have to *promise* never to bring it up again, or act like you're thinking about it." "Oh," says the boy. "It's fine," says the girl, "everything is going to be fine." The boy says, "Okay." "You like me, don't you?" asks the girl. "Yes," says the boy. "Good. Because I like you," says the girl. "Do you like me a lot?" The boy says, "Yes." The girl smiles. "I'm going to kiss you now," the girl says. "What are we doing today, when it gets light?" asks the boy. "We'll sleep through the light," says the girl, "but later I'll invite everyone out. We will go back there. All our friends will buy you a drink." "That sounds nice," says the boy. The girl leans nearer to the boy; she reaches out her left hand to touch him.

The boy quickly opens the backseat door and tumbles out of the car.

I can feel him finding me without knowing; it is because he is centripetal. The city has been dark for so long—the whole night and longer—but not real dark, just a kind of endless, shrugging, lighted darkness. It's a dim glowing darkness and always has been. The boy is running. Covered in the grit of the road, he is running away from the chauffeured town car that the girl sits in; he is heading into the center. The air screams a message, saying, *Hello, happy birthday!* The whole clunky poetics of his disaster is a birthday party and he is running into it. His legs are sinking ships, his eyes are diamonds, and his heart is bitter inertia as he searches for an arrival. He is making turns into the night, propelling himself dumbly with determined exasperation, and the streetlamps sing fluorescently. He's racing. He doesn't want to be late for his own birthday party. He can't breathe. His lungs dissolve. The world turns red. And there I am.

The boy with black hair and a pale face finally stops because he sees me standing in a patch of spotlighted grass under the final streetlamp on earth. "Oh," he says, breathless, "I found you." I stay where I am; he limps at me, walking into my circle of light. He moves with caution, maybe shame, and familiarity. The only things to say are the simplest. "You disappeared," I say. "You left one day and didn't come back." "But here we are," he says. "But it doesn't matter," I say. We are asunder, looking at each other; he's not coming any closer. "You're dirty," I say. "It's because I jumped out of a car," he says. "That was stupid of you," I say. "I'm not good at apologies," he says. "I don't want you to apologize," I say, "is what you have to understand now." "You're probably not really here, anyway," he tells me. "You're all wrong," I say. "And you took the game belly." "I know," he says. "The one precious thing," I say. "Yes," he says. "And you destroyed it," I say. "What if I say it's complicated?" he asks. "Why would you do what you did?" I ask. "I'm not sure," he says. "You're too lazy to find it out," I say. "Maybe I should change," he says. "Do it somewhere," I say. "With you?" he asks, leaning. "No," I say. "On the fluffy chair?" he asks. "Never there," I say. "I don't know where." He says, "Maybe I'm beyond help." "That could be," I say. "But maybe I'm not," he says. We are silent and can hear the manic noise of a generator tumbling into itself somewhere nearby—it sounds like lovely music. An owl, an unlikely creature, lands on the streetlamp we stand under in my circle of light; it watches us with reflective eyes, maybe judging. "There's an owl," says the boy, looking up. "I won't forget to wish you happy birthday," I say, "so happy birthday." "I miss you, I think," he says. He looks anxious; I know he wants there to be something else to do, or some mechanism that could solve the problem of the wreck of our convergences. If I know anything about this, I know the pathetic glow of his desire. I've been that intimate with his grammar.

MILK

The horse was in the kitchen. I sat before warm cereal and noted it suspiciously. It whinnied and clacked its shoes on the tile. It remained wedged in the space between the refrigerator and the counter where the microwave hung. My brother entered the room and slunk into the animal without recognizing it. The horse barked once but did not otherwise react. The stupid boy fell deliriously backward and landed on his spine. He glared vacuously from the floor, uncomprehending, and a frustrated wail grew out of his pink throat. His tantrums were systematic rituals and his primary form of articulation. The helpless pulchritude of the outbursts, the compositional concision of his fugues, was unrealized by his family and violently controverted by me. I scowled at him from my seat, cursing the scapegrace for his idiocy and the horse for having been there. The ruckus prompted our father frowningly in from the living room. "Shut up!" I yelped at the relative on the floor. My father's glare angled over to me at the breakfast table. His face was cancerously grim. "Don't," he issued toward me; presently he transferred his attention down to my brother and again remonstrated, "Don't," and then he tilted his blockish head up at the horse and said, "Get." After that he left the room. I can't remember what happened next. My brother's fits always wound

83

down—inevitably through our mother's tired comforting. The horse yet kept stubbornly in place. I was old enough to know how to tie my shoes and read a clock, but couldn't do either; I wore penny loafers with pennies shoved in them and was unpunctual. After exhausting myself on the swing set nailed to a dead tree in the backyard, I returned that afternoon to the kitchen for a glass of milk; to my chagrin the horse remained, preventing my way to the refrigerator. I went after the maid, Cindy Crawford. She was an emaciated Amish child bride my family employed to tend to chores and substitute as my caretaker when required. I found her in the laundry room of the basement: her thin arms were stuck in the soapy water of the deep washbowl by the hamper. She was scrubbing determinedly at some submerged article. "Cindy," I said. She concentrated at her task, but soon pulled her hands out of the basin; she clutched a small pair of briefs with fecal stains the color of dark loam. I demanded her attention again. The room was unfinished, with gray cement walls and mildewed corners; there was one smeary bit of window, at the ceiling over the hamper, that viewed a gutter clogged with dead leaves of anterior seasons, which emitted nominal sunshine. Cindy was plain: maybe with a long visage, and straight nose, and black hair always resigned to a starched cap. I didn't care for her enough to be damaged by her emotionally, but she was convenient. "The horse's in front of the milk," I told her, "make it shoo." She listened dully before she dumped the soiled laundry into the brown water of the washbowl and followed me through the basement and upstairs. Cindy inspected the problem and looked at me nervously. "I have no truck with your father's horse," she whispered. "I want some milk," I insisted. She turned to the horse again and I thought she would cry. My mother arrived home from an errand and came in through the mudroom by the garage. "What is that

84

creature still doing in here!" she complained. "I'm sorry, Mrs.," warbled Cindy. "Well it isn't your fault—is it?" my mother said. Cindy shook her head ashamedly. My mother crossed her arms over her bosom, ergo the fabric of her floral-patterned shirt bunched. "It's only been there all day. It's going to take a doo doo on my floor pretty soon, I expect," she said. She scowled at us, and then at the horse, and finally she quit the room. I pulled on Cindy's homely dress, which ended at her ankles and had no buttons. "You can have sink water for now," she offered. "But I want a glass of milk!" I said. Cindy paled with upset. "Nothing doing," she whispered. "I don't *want* sink water!" I said. She was silent for a while. Finally she spoke. "I'm sorry," she said. I didn't know enough to recognize her earnestness. She touched my hair gently. I had no love for her. I didn't know how to make love. I left to sulk; when I came back I had missed the information to properly contextualize how my father came to resolve the matter of the stubborn horse by fetching a handgun, which I had been ignorant to the existence of, from some unfamiliar cranny of the house, and sticking the muzzle against the animal's skull before he discharged several bullets in there with rude-sounding pops that spattered sneezes of blood across the door of the microwave. The horse screamed like a teenage girl, but once, and collapsed unceremoniously. Its bulk weighted down on its splayed legs; its head caught on the counter's edge, with tongue crept weirdly through its teeth. As he examined the corpse, I was transfixed upon my father's back: wrinkled flannel tucked into sweatpants, thick splotchy neck and balding pate, dark scabs behind the lobe of one red ear. He stuck the firearm into a pocket, which began to sag from the weight, exposing a corner of his briefs. "There," he said. He was a taciturn man when I knew him. He never spoke of it but he had killed villages of gooks in the war, distanced by a plane full of nifty bombs. Mother arrived to assert her displeasure. "What an utter mess," she groaned. "That beast was impossible—how'd it get in this morning? Why wasn't it in the stable where it should of been, Edward?" My father blushed with anger. "Don't antagonize me!" he yelled. My mother scoffed. "I am doing no such thing. Now: how do you plan to get rid of it? And you better believe I want it out pretty darn quick!" She didn't remain for an answer. My father stared accusatorily at Cindy and me before he stomped away withal. I went to the corpse and prodded its tense ribs. I never saw the old man kill something that big again. By morrow he was pouring gasoline into a hornet's nest in the ground near the swing set, and he came to murder a family cat when I was teenaged, but this became a singular incident more disturbing in my memory for lack of an objective correlative. Cindy gave me a glass of milk and then went to the attic to feed the grandparents. At dusk a dirty truck drove up our hill and Ingvar, the savant handyman my father employed, helped lug the corpse out the house to the little wooden stable at the edge of the property, whereat they commenced to harvest the body for meat that Ingvar took home to his motel room for pay. I saw them carry the gutted remains, in slices wrapped partly in blue plastic tarp, to the bed of the parked truck. My father instructed Ingvar to dump what he didn't want off at the municipal landfill, by the pile of rock salt, to be left for the birds and coyotes. "That horse was nothing but a pain in the neck," my mother said at supper. My father winced and ejaculated an overstated sigh. We ate meatloaf and broccoli and drank tall glasses of milk. The television, carted in from the living room, played the evening news at low volume following our required prayer. The stable thereafter was a shed. Father bought a new riding lawn mower he kept in there. The name of the horse was Black Beauty even though it was brown.

BURNING CHURCH

MONDAY

A television was stuck on top of the shelf that ran along the cloudy windows that looked out to the soccer field and pine trees beyond; ignored chemistry textbooks leaned in a pile on one side of it and a purposeless stuffed animal was abandoned on the other side. The faculty lounge was yellow and gray; the air smelt of stale coffee. The French teacher sat unoccupied on the threadbare couch. She slid her feet on the tile and her shoes squeaked. She stopped when she noticed. The television was turned on, but the dust that coated the screen from want of use was undisturbed except for three accidental traces of fingers. Burning Church stood at the counter by the sink where the percolator was, acting undecided. He glanced at the French teacher who was watching the mute television turned to a news channel. He moved slightly and inspected the percolator. He reached out and touched it. He coughed, and then winced at that, and quickly grabbed the percolator, and grabbed a Styrofoam cup nearby, and nervously poured himself a cup of coffee. He brought the cup to his face and inhaled the scent. He peeked at the tray holding packets of sugar, sweetener, and tiny plastic cups of nondairy creamer. He turned toward where the French teacher sat on the couch. She wasn't watching the television but staring at him amazed. He paused guiltily holding the cup near his chin. He needed to look away from her, and did, and glanced opportunistically at the mute television. He saw footage of a plane careering into a thin characterless building and exploding. The footage only lasted a moment, but repeated constantly. He looked from the television on top of the shelf that ran along the windows to the old couch where the French teacher sat, looking at him, and he grinned and shrugged. He shuffled around quickly and grabbed at the sugar packets. "What kind of people do you suppose we are, Burning?" he heard the French teacher ask. He tore open two sugar packets simultaneously and poured the sugar into his cup of stale coffee. "In apropos of—?" he muttered. He picked up a tiny cup of non-dairy creamer and introduced it to his coffee. "I mean, well, I'm a positive thinker and I believe that, even when there is so much ambiguousness about us that's hard to explain all the way, we all are loving people fundamentally," she said. Burning glanced at her, picked up two more packets of sugar, and tore both. The opened packets stuck between his thumb and forefinger above the mouth of his cup. "Mr. Church, that sure is a lot of sugar for your coffee," the French teacher said. Burning coughed. "I can't face my tenth graders otherwise," he said. The French teacher giggled curtly and loud; he looked at her over his shoulder and saw she was watching the television screen again. "Don't you think love is integral?" she asked distractedly. Burning let the packets' contents drop altogether in his coffee. "Um," he said. He picked up a stray plastic spoon and stirred his drink around. "Forgive me if I'm speaking out of turn, but I always suspected you to be a *lonely* man," said the French teacher. Burning turned, holding cup, leaned on the sticky counter that poked into the flesh of his back. The

French teacher was a mannerly but fraught seeming woman whose lack of makeup made her look stubbornly creased in the face, with especial folds anxiously at her eyes and the corners of her thin mouth. She watched the television; she wrung her hands but stopped when she noticed. Burning knew she was married to somebody. He thought they might be the kind of marrieds with a skinny mirror in the bathroom directly opposite the toilet so that everybody sitting on the toilet was confronted with the reflection of herself there. He thought she might be the kind of woman apt to be vaguely indescribably troubled if, through some chance mention, she learned that Burning slept on a single mattress without sheets, tucked in the corner of his bedroom floor, with only a lining of yellowed newspaper underneath it. He opened his mouth slightly. The French teacher watched the plane careen endlessly into the salty-white building and explode. She tilted her head. "Are you, Mr. Church, without a love to call yours?" she asked lightly. "I don't, well," stammered Burning. He shifted his weight about. "I keep to myself mostly," he concluded. The French teacher peered at him. A few drops of rain smacked across the wide windows. The clouds over the soccer field were heavily purplish. "You know," said the French teacher, "these days there's no *shame* in trying one's hand at Internet dating." Mr. Burning felt as if he would blush. "I know several people, as a matter of fact, who have met their soul mates that way and you'd be surprised to know who," she said. Burning sipped his coffee and bitterly choked on it. "I'm sorry," said the French teacher, "but did you mention whether you thought we're all good at heart, or no?" The intercom mounted above the door by the clock clucked unexpectedly. A voice recognizable as the plump secretary's, from the main office, blurted, "Why do they hate us?" There was a crude static rasp and nothing else was heard. "Did you just say something?" asked the French teacher. She was watching the screen again. "I said it sounds like Audrey leaned on the intercom button again," said Burning, and he walked hurriedly to the door and out into the hallway, closing the door behind him. He looked at his coffee, and frowned, and drank it. A child was curled up on the floor under a hallway water fountain crying hysterically. Her face was contorted, and glimmering wetly, and red. He stood, holding his coffee, and stared at her. She looked a few grades below high school. What is she doing here? he thought. A young monitor was watching her from the doorway of the computer lab. Burning Church swallowed the hallway air and walked to his classroom. He felt empty and restless. Outside was darkening from storm and rain streaks punctuated the windows of his room that looked over the muddy student parking lot downhill. His cold coffee was uncomfortable. He stood in his shadowy room waiting. Then he sat down at his desk. He heard a gang of students noisily pass in the hallway. Then he heard an electric hum and the prattling rain.

TUESDAY

He remembered the year of the murder and frowned. He stood leaning against clutter in the small closet at the end of the hall that the English department used as a storage room. He looked at Howard Lately. Howard Lately sat childishly on the radiator. The radiator was old and heavy, not attached to anything. Burning Church coughed. He didn't say anything. He blinked. He said, "Will you help me?" Howard cracked his neck hard. "Ow," Howard said. He did it again. He twisted his head sideways; his neck flesh wrinkled and Burning heard a bodily internal crunch. Burning looked at the piles of musty books that lined the wooden shelves in the room. He picked one up. The title was worn off the spine. The smell of the book made him sneeze. "Well," said Burning. "And his parents are here?" asked Howard. Burning rubbed the book he held, rubbed the dust on it slightly, and displaced it. He set it back to the shelf. He kept looking at it. "The kid who killed the other kid that year was your student," said Burning. Howard rubbed his eyes vigorously. "A taciturn boy," Howard said. He opened his eyes and looked at Burning. His eyes were pink with tiny veins. He looked bored. "None of what you'd call warning signs, you know, the taciturnity exempt—but some *are* quiet. So what? Some are just quiet. Some are a lot of things and they don't hurt anybody," said Howard. Burning looked into the long fluorescent light above him. He looked back at Howard with colors floating in his vision. "Did he like the subject?" asked Burning. Howard hummed thoughtfully. "He did his work," he concluded. "There was nothing in it that in hindsight suggested—?" asked Burning. Howard put a finger to an eye. "Suggested he'd murder? Like I said, who's to say? He had A's with me, but was unexceptional. His dad owned a Glock. All the world's a stage . . ." said Howard. He took out a handkerchief and dabbed an eye. "I wonder how he feels about it now, that kid," he said. "You think he thinks somebody should have realized? Realized something was wrong and helped him?" asked Burning. Howard looked at his handkerchief, folded it. "What do you think is wrong with this kid?" he asked. "Your kid with the parents here or on the way." Burning stirred slightly. "Oh, he's probably borderline. It's not prudent for me to make that judgment," he said. Howard stood up. The radiator wobbled, groaning. He dusted the seat of his pants. "It's always something," he said. He walked out of the room slowly without another word for Burning. Burning lingered in the sultry dust temporarily and then stepped back into the hallway. The hallway was empty; most students left after classes. He walked quickly to the main office. He paused out front of the main office. He went inside. The plump secretary sat at the front desk, glaring at a computer screen. Burning hesitated, waited to be noticed. He cleared his throat. His hand left his pocket. He scratched his ear. The secretary looked up casually and started when she saw him there. "Oh Burning!" she said. He thought she looked like a frog and that that was endearing. He wondered about her. "Didn't notice you," she said. Burning heard a sudden boyish chirp behind him. He turned around startled. His student Vowel Shift sat there. The student languished uncomfortably in a chair with a felt seat; he leaned back and pressed his head tightly against the wall. "Hello, Mr. Church," said Vowel. He looked ghostly and unhappy. "Hello, Vowel," said Burning, but almost whispered. "How are you?" asked the student. "I'm well, thanks," said Burning. Vowel tried to smile disastrously. "Everything is going to be okay, Vowel," said Burning. Vowel looked at nothing. "I'm so tired," he said. Burning didn't know what that meant. He turned around and saw the plump secretary leaning strenuously over the desk and holding a thick file at him. "Oh," he said, grabbed it. The secretary collapsed back into her seat and her seat whistled. "Mr. and Mrs. Shift are in the interior conference room," she said. "Okay," Burning said. The file was heavy; he grasped it cautiously. He expected the contents. He turned and glanced at Vowel. The boy looked sort of condemned. "I'm not ashamed of anything I wrote," he said, downcast at the drab carpet, "but anyway, I can't help it." Burning opened his mouth and made a little sound. He didn't say anything. He turned around and walked away. He walked further into the main office until he stood outside the interior conference room, the door with frosted glass. He went in. The square table in the room was large, the color of newsprint. An old couple sat at one end and the school psychologist, Len Cardinal, was put smilingly across from them. Len Cardinal just finished a sentence. The walls were decorated with incidental posters. The old couple and Len Cardinal turned and looked at Burning when he came in. He stood there holding the thick file. Len Cardinal sat with an identical file open before him; the old couple had one too. "Hello, Burning," said Len Cardinal. "Please have a seat." He pointed to a chair next to him. Burning went and sat there. "This is Mr. Church, Vowel's creative writing instructor," said Len Cardinal to the old couple. He pointed to the old couple. "Burning, may I introduce Gerund and Beatrice, Vowel's parents," he said. Burning inspected them across the gray table. They looked tried, circumstantially displeased. Gerund grimaced at Burning and then, reflexively, glanced guiltily at the closed file in front of him. "How do you, Mr. Church?" whispered Beatrice. "Burning, please," said Burning. "Mr. Church," barked Gerund, nodding tersely. "I just want to," said Burning, touching the file he put before him, "preface my entrance into this conversation by saying that Vowel is in no way in trouble." He looked at the parents, but they did not belie responses. "He hasn't done anything against the rules," he said, "but as I'm sure Len has explained, we have to take these matters seriously these days." Len Cardinal nodded in solidarity. "The environment of public education has changed greatly over the years," Len Cardinal said. Burning wanted coffee. "Not too long ago a student here brought a weapon to school and killed a peer," said Burning. "Tragedies like that may be prevented if we responsibly address areas of, um, concern." "You think my son's going to kill someone?" Gerund said in a sort of uncontrolled yelp that made Burning shiver. "That's, that's not what this is about, really. I'm just saying . . . clarifying the context we have to treat this in," Burning managed. Len Cardinal smiled defensively through a heavy but brief general silence. "Your son is sort of brilliant," Burning whispered. Len Cardinal bent forward a little. "Everybody thinks Vowel is just so sharp," he said, looking between Burning and the parents. Gerund winced suspiciously. "Well he's doing something he ought not to, obviously. Don't treat me daft, I'm not. I read this—all this. It's filth! What kind of writing class is this, anyway?" He pushed the file before him away angrily. Burning looked down at the file he had and opened it. The file contained copies of every story Vowel wrote for his creative writing elective. "I'm not here to argue the quality of the assignments," said Burning. "Honestly, I think they're very strong. They're just, well, full of what might be seen as red flags. Thematically they seem to suggest Vowel might be having some emotional problems. Also, his relationship with you may be . . . a matter for further attention." Burning blinked. Gerund was blushing uneasily. Beatrice looked folded, overwrought. "It's just stories," she blurted. Burning turned to Len Cardinal. Len Cardinal smiled and coughed into his fist. "Sometimes a student's work expresses certain things that he can't otherwise say about his life," he told the parents. Burning flipped through the pages in the file. "Almost every piece is about a sexually confused young man who feels like his home environment is so hostile he somehow acts out with rage or reckless and self-destructive behavior," he said. "Oh for crying out loud," cried Beatrice, "what about the story with the giraffes? It's giraffes!" Burning frowned. "I believe the family of giraffes can be read as a metaphor for your family," he said. "Well that's just silly," said Beatrice. She grabbed the file near her. "And who's to say he's writing about himself and about us, anyway? I don't see it. It's just stories. He's kind of creative, he likes to make up little scenes. Maybe some of them are a little crude. But why does the giraffe family have to be us? If Vowel's writing about himself, where is all this stuff about 'sexual confusion' coming from? Vowel's an assembled boy; he's normal with a good head on his shoulders. If you can't see that—" she said. Burning tried to interrupt her, but when she stopped he stammered and said nothing. Gerund buried his face in his wrinkled hands and groaned. "There's the suicide," Burning said finally. "There we go," Len Cardinal nodded. Burning picked some stories out of the file, set them before him delicately. "For instance, the giraffe son in the giraffe family commits suicide by refusing to eat leaves," he said, "and here in this one the young prince dies when he disguises himself as a lion and the king unknowingly shoots him during a hunting expedition. He wanted his father to feel remorse for being so emotionally unavailable and attached to the values of the court, which the young prince found suffocating." "Is there a point to this? Is our son going to kill somebody or not? Or is he going to kill himself? Do we need to send him somewhere, are you saying?" growled Gerund. Burning stared at him; then looked at his wife. He held one of the stories, printed on crisp paper and stapled in the corner, indefinitely in his hand, but didn't notice. He thought about Vowel Shift sitting pressing himself against the wall of the main office. Vowel was in the eleventh grade. The stories were well written, he thought. But what was the boy going to do, he asked himself, and what was he supposed to do, really? He didn't know well enough. He looked at the old couple. He was holding a piece of work, he noticed then: the story about the prince. He had given the fiction an A grade, as he had all the rest by Vowel, but also sent it to Len Cardinal. He put the story down. He looked at his shadow on the pale table's surface. The boy should be okay, he thought. He wanted that, anyway. Len Cardinal was waiting for him to speak. He gulped some air then.

WEDNESDAY

The faculty dining room was congested and brown with old drapes. Burning sat simply across the greasy table from the principal. The principal filled a suit that was just perceptibly too snug. They both ate diminutive servings of meatloaf from Styrofoam trays, using plastic forks. The principal farted; he kept his head down and didn't acknowledge it. Burning sucked air in his mouth. His hand moved toward the cup of coffee near to his tray. He picked up the cup and moved it to his lips. A little steam rose out of the coffee, across his nose. He looked down into the cup. "Get that in the snack line?" asked the principal. Burning looked over his cup at him. He was near shoveling a bit of meatloaf into his throat. His eyes watched Burning back. "Um, yeah," said Burning; he lowered the cup down from his mouth. "All right?" asked the principal. "It's tolerable," Burning answered. The principal held out his unoccupied hand expectantly. Burning looked at him. The principal didn't move. Burning picked his cup back up and handed it across the table. The principal accepted and grabbed the cup; he took a sip of it. He smacked his lips thoughtfully, handed the cup back quick. "That's shit," he said. He frowned. Burning kept the cup shyly in front of him. The principal said, "The new vendor this year *insisted* we do coffee and they don't even have the decency to provide a good blend." He put a stained paper napkin on his lips. Burning set his cup down again. "The kids probably don't mind it," he said. "Yeah, no, they just want the caffeine," said the principal. A fly landed close to Burning's tray. His hand rested on the greasy table's surface and kind of stuck there. He raised his hand and the fly left. His skin felt gummy. "Of course there have been complaints," said the principal. He clutched the plastic fork yet. He sighed dramatically. "What do you think, Burning?" he asked. Burning's brow furrowed. He tried to think. "About letting the kids have coffee, what do you think?" the principal asked again. Burning replied, "Oh, I don't know. I don't have an opinion. Maybe it helps, maybe it makes things worse . . . I'm not sure." Burning picked up the cup and inspected the coffee inside as an excuse to sip at it. There could be more sugar, he thought. He wasn't particular about coffee. "What I told the vendor was to tell those employees working the snack line never to sell more than one cup to the same kid in one day," said the principal. "That's reasonable," said Burning. The principal wagged his head. "It's ineffectual," he sighed. "If a kid wants more he just asks a friend to get it." "Oh, right," Burning said. The principal ate noncommittally for a while. Burning watched him hunched over and masticating. He felt it was unfortunate, the trivial considerations the principal was responsible for. Things that mattered less were consequential. The principal was good at the struggle. He had held his position for longer than Burning had taught there. He hired Burning, actually. Burning heard he had been the vice-principal before he became the principal. He was married but had no children. Nobody talked about it. "Has there been as much trouble with the coffee as with the old soda machine?" Burning asked finally. The principal looked up tensely. His knuckles whitened on the hand holding the plastic fork. He said, with a mouthful, "Decidedly no! Nothing quite that catastrophic." He swallowed food. He said, "It might get there if one of those problem moms picks up her daughter and the kid's absolutely wired, but we learned a thing or two from the soda machine debacle." He put more food inside his mouth. He said, "But thanks for reminding me of that highlight of my career." He laughed painfully. "I'm sorry," said Burning. The principal wiped his hand through the stale air. "It's okay. I was trying to repress the memory of all the agony and embarrassment that soda machine caused me, is all. I swear, sometimes I feel like pulling a Mrs. Ferguson!" Burning looked at him blankly. He waited for anything else. The principal didn't offer additional explanation; he readdressed his tray. He ate again with his head down. Burning sat confused and wanting. He looked at the principal pleadingly but was ignored. "What's a Mrs. Ferguson?" he asked dubiously. The principal looked up at him. He smiled with a spot of food resting on a wet tooth. "You *know* . . ." he said. With one hand he made a gesture in front of Burning's face as if to clarify his meaning. It looked like he was tightening a noose around his neck. Momentarily the tip of his thick tongue stuck out the corner of his mouth. He went back to eating again. Burning blushed in the upsetting silence between them. Finally he spoke. "Who is Mrs. Ferguson?" he begged. The principal groped conclusively at his tray and clucked. He set his fork down on the table. Particles of dull meat fell off the fork and collected inconsequentially on the table. He smiled devilishly at Burning. "That poor bitch you replaced all those years ago," he said, "may she rest in peace—or *pieces*, considering the circumstances." He looked conspiratorial, but Burning was lost. "What about her, exactly? I don't quite get your meaning," Burning said. The principal's face sagged instantly; he leaned back careful in his chair and the chair creaked plastically. "Gosh, I'm sorry, Burning. I shouldn't make light of that incident, yeah? That was a real inappropriate joke." Burning opened his mouth dumbly. He felt like crying. "I really have no idea what you're talking about," he stammered. The principal sighed relieved, unwound. "All is forgiven?" he asked. "What—?" asked Burning. The principal grabbed his tray suddenly and pushed his chair back. He stood up. "Nice lunching with you, Burning," he said, smiling. He turned, walked, and threw his tray out in the garbage near to the door. Then he left. Burning was alone in the faculty dining room and at the greasy table. He looked at his remaining meal. He saw the principal's abandoned fork across the table.

THURSDAY

The light outside, coming through the windows, drably substituted for the long fluorescent bulbs overheard, kept off. His classroom was vacant, complicated by gregarious shadows. Burning sat behind his desk. He heard distant sounds of cars starting then driving up the dirt hill out of the student parking lot, away from school. He stared across the dim room at the clunky television set mounted from the ceiling in the far corner. The screen was lit with awkward outside light, but the television was turned on and he squinted at it. The sound was muted; the channel was news. Without looking, Burning stuck his hand out and moved it across the desk's surface. He felt for the remote. He grabbed at it where it was on top of an empty case for a videocassette. He picked it up and held it in the air before him, pointed at the hanging set. He pushed a button and closed captioning appeared at the bottom of the screen. He lowered his arm and with his hand let the remote set on the desk again, but not where he had put it before. The news channel broadcasted footage from a military plane dropping bombs on an indistinct surface. The image was distorted by pixilation. He saw grayish shapes moving and bursts of sickly light. He squinted harder to read the closed captioning at the screen's bottom. It hurt his eyes to squint. He tried to remember the last time he went to the mall for an eye exam. He probably needed an updated lens prescription. He took his glasses off and put them back on. He looked at the television screen, suspended and bathed weakly in outside light; he saw ambiguous pixels. He didn't like going to the mall. He picked up the remote, unthinking. He held up the remote again. He pointed it at the set; nothing happened. His arm fell limp again. He put the remote atop student papers. He sat still and looked at the television. There was a significant instant tendency. He almost understood it was noise, quick, exclamatory: like a tree's trunk snapping. He was senseless, rattled. And a following metal crash. He started at the crash. The television broke to pieces when it hit the tile ground. Burning was unresponsive. The sound of the crash was not singular, but orchestral. It stunned his reason. Presently the teacher from the neighbor classroom pressed her body nervously through his doorway. She peered at the source of the crash that caused her hurrying over. Some thin wires hung taut from the hole in the ceiling down to where the set had landed. She turned blurrily to Burning. Burning was upright and still; he finally turned to see her. "Cheryl," he said. "What on earth?" she gasped. Burning looked at her. Her one hand grabbed the doorframe. He turned again and looked over his desk at the fallen set. "My television," he recognized. Cheryl stood unfamiliarly. She did nothing. Burning waited. She decided to lean forward and flick on the overheard fluorescent lights. The room turned shallowly bright and Burning squinted. The felled wreck was most apparent in the disinterested fluorescent light. "Are you okay?" asked Cheryl. "Um, yes," said Burning. He squinted at her. "I'm a little . . ." he said. "What *happened?*" Cheryl cried.

Burning leaned into his seat. "I don't really know," he said shyly. "Somebody could have been seriously hurt," said Cheryl. He thought she sounded offended. "I realize that," he told her. "Well," she said, "what now?" "Don't worry," he said. She stepped backward. "I'll get the janitor," Burning said. "Is that all?" she asked. "I'll let somebody know," said Burning. Cheryl leaned into the hall and looked at the doorway to her room. "What about *my* set?" she asked. "What?" said Burning. She turned back. "Is it safe?" she asked. "Somebody can check it," said Burning. "Well I won't go near it," she said. "Okay," said Burning. "Be careful in here," she said. "Everything is fine," he said. She went. Burning stood up. He looked at the television in parts on the floor. He walked out of the room and went for the janitor. The janitor sat in his dingy office by the bathrooms by the gym. The door was stuck ajar. Burning put his head in. The janitor was sitting at his cluttered old desk. One bright lamp shined on the desk. The janitor wore a greasy uniform. He was occupied looking inside a radio. He did not notice Burning poke his head into the office. Burning stared at him and came fully into the room. The janitor looked up. An instrument folded in his hand paused inside the radio. "Yeah?" the janitor said. Burning looked away from him. The walls were covered by rusty shelves full with miscellany. The air smelled pleasant. "I'm sorry, Matthias, but I have a problem," said Burning. The janitor frowned at him. "Come here," he said. Burning went to him. He stood by the desk at the edge of the lamp's light. The janitor looked up at him. "See this?" he said. He gestured at the radio with his instrument. Burning looked down at the radio, the back of which, removed, showed the insides. He saw mechanics he didn't understand. "This is a cunt," said Matthias. "Oh," said Burning. "They don't make them like this no more," said Matthias. Burning gulped. His throat was dry. Matthias looked down into the radio. "It was mother's," he said. "Looks complicated," Burning said. "She's gone now," said Matthias. Burning scratched his nose. Matthias set down the instrument. The angle of the lamp's light made the inside of the radio look depthless. "What is memory?" asked Matthias. "Uh," said Burning, "my television fell . . . and crashed." Matthias wouldn't look up. "It's broke then," he said. "It just fell for no reason," said Burning. "When I was a little boy my mother would buy me a milkshake every Sunday," said Matthias. He turned the radio in the light, kept looking into it. "There's got to be something in here that can make sense of all of this," he said. He held the radio between his two palms. Burning leaned over. "Maybe it's not what it does so much as the shape of things," said Matthias. He let go. He wiped a hand on his leg. He looked up at Burning. Burning leaned back. Matthias reached to the lamp and shined it on him. "The both of us is going to have to file some paperwork for what's been done," he said. Burning stood in the bright lamp's light. "Come this way," said Matthias. He prepared to stand up. The chair moaned.

FRIDAY

The hallway had a flickering light; the tiles shined darkly. Burning Church walked toward the end. Some of the classroom doors were stuck ajar. He glanced casually in rooms he passed. The history teacher with the room on the left was on leave. He glanced into her room incidentally. Burning Church caught sight of somebody taking a poster off the wall. He stopped, turned around, peered in again. The history teacher's girlfriend was holding the poster. She curled it up and put it in one of the cardboard boxes that were set on unoccupied student desks. The history teacher's substitute stood behind the classroom desk watching. Burning paused and watched. The history teacher's girlfriend realized she was being watched from the flickering hall; she caught her hands around herself and turned to Burning indecipherably. Burning was startled. She looked closer and her glare softened. "Mr. Church!" she cried. She put her hand to her mouth guiltily. "I'm sorry. Hi," said Burning. There was silence between them. "Am I intruding?" Burning asked. The woman breathed. "No," she said. The substitute teacher regarded Burning. Burning did nothing. "Come in," said the history teacher's girlfriend. Burning considered her. Her name was Esther. Burning stepped into the classroom. She came to him, threw her arms at him. The embrace was unexpected. Burning felt she hugged him for a considerable time. He did know her. He met her first at a lawn social three years ago. Last year he accepted a dinner invitation at her house with the history teacher. She let him go. "What are you doing?" asked Burning. "I don't know," Esther coughed. Burning looked at the cardboard boxes on the student desks. The substitute teacher slunk back. She chewed on her fingers. Burning didn't know her name. He looked at Esther. Her eyes were shaded. They didn't say anything. "How are you?" asked Burning. "I'm not supposed to be here," she said. She held her face. "Where is Lucretia?" asked Burning. Esther looked at the light. "At home," she said. Burning stood. Esther didn't look at him. Nothing happened and Burning felt unsure. Finally Esther spoke again. "I'm just here to take care of some things," she said. "That's nice," said Burning. He clucked his tongue. "I haven't seen you in so long," he said. Esther sighed unevenly. "I hope everything is . . ." said Burning. Esther looked at him. "It hasn't been announced yet," she said. She didn't move, except her mouth trembled. "What?" said Burning. Esther turned her hands around. She didn't say anything. "Lucretia isn't coming back," she said. The baby was coming later, Burning thought. "She's not coming back," Burning said. "What is she doing?" Esther was breathless. She surveyed the room. "Almost done," she said. "What's the matter?" asked Burning. "Do you see anything that maybe I don't see that belongs to Lucretia that I haven't packed yet that I need to pack or it will get left here?" she asked. Burning looked around the room. "Oh—that print of Washington crossing the Delaware," he said. Esther saw it on the wall. "Who painted that, anyway?" she said. "That's hers," Burning said. Esther went to it, plucked it from the wall. "I've never seen this before. Maybe she won't want it," she said. "She won't want it?" Burning asked. Esther held the print inexplicably. She said, "I don't *know*, I . . . I don't know what to take, what to leave, what to throw out! She didn't *say*. I just . . ." Burning tucked his chin into his throat. "What's the matter, Esther?" he asked. She didn't move. "I'm intruding," he said. He turned to walk out. Esther threw the print into a cardboard box. The glass frame cracked and the substitute started with a croak. Esther looked at Burning. "Something went wrong," she said. The hallway light flickered constantly. "With," she said. Burning reached out. His arm stayed suspended and useless. "She didn't *tell* me what she wanted," Esther said, "just that I had to come in her place to take her things because she can't come back, our, Burning, our child is, I don't know, and she won't talk to me about it, so here I am, I'm at a loss, you know." She stared into Burning. "I mean I know how it happened. It's not supposed to but it did. But she's so distant about it and what am I supposed to do? I don't know what to do because she could be close to me about it but this is something else we didn't expect and it's just, just, maybe just," she said. Burning couldn't respond. He watched her eyes change. "She was sitting on the toilet, really," she said. There was something universal about her eyes. "Well," Burning said. Esther came closer. She put her lips near his face. "I don't know why I'm telling you this," she whispered, "but I told her to start medicine. I don't know what I'm even *saying*. If it's the right thing or not . . . and who's to say because a doctor will just give it to her. That's what doctors do, right? Who's to say why this happened or what now we do." She backed away from him. Her hand landed on the mouth of a cardboard box situated on a student desk. "I shouldn't lose my composure," she said. Burning opened his mouth. "It's hard to speak," he said. Esther didn't look away from him. "She quit," she said. "What then?" asked Burning. "Um," said Esther, "I guess we'll move? To another district? I don't know." She pawed the box distractedly. "What can I do?" asked Burning. Esther looked toward the inert, unnameable substitute teacher; she looked back. "Will you . . . will you help me carry a box down to my car?" she asked. "Of course," said Burning. He moved suddenly, picked a box up. "Is it heavy?" asked Esther. "No," he said. He looked down into the box and saw the broken frame. Esther picked up a box. "Okay," she said. They left the room. The hallway light flickered. Burning blinked. "The thing about the world," said Esther, "is that it goes around and around. Is that right?" Burning walked next to her toward the end of the hallway and the staircase to the right. "I don't know," he said. "That's what they say, anyway," she said. They walked down the staircase, to the parking lot. Esther's car was a purple minivan. She set her box down on the sunny asphalt and took keys out from her pocket. She opened the van's gate. "There," she said. Burning set down the box he carried in the back of the van. He reached over, picked the other box up, and put it in the back of the van. Esther shut the van's gate. She tossed her keys lightly in her palm. "It was nice to see you, Burning," she said downwardly. "Okay," said Burning. Esther looked at him. "I mean it," she said. Burning said nothing. He looked at the sun. He looked at her standing there. "You and Lucretia," he said. He closed his mouth. She waited unmoving. "I love you," he said. She blinked wetly. "Around and around unstoppable," she said. "Is it going to be all right?" asked Burning. Esther smiled and it hurt to look at.

SATURDAY

He ate at the food court in the mall. He went there because it was awkward sitting in a restaurant alone. He couldn't make a meal because he didn't feel like grocery shopping. He sat at a table by himself at the food court with crowded tables of families and teenagers around him. The families looked fat and sad. The teenagers looked terrified of themselves. He dreaded running out of food at home. He looked at his plastic plate of steamed vegetables and chicken. He touched the plate; it moved stubbornly across the table as he pushed it. The table was filmy. He drank coffee. The coffee in the paper cup was next to the plate, the thin napkin he had. He rested his hand on the napkin, not the table's surface. He remembered when the food court was closed for a while. He hunched over his plate of food. There was a retailer selling video games near his table. He heard passersby talking, the same as each other. His glasses were foggy with prints; he didn't notice in the unremarkable light in the mall. He looked up. He looked back down at the table, at his plate of food there. He forked vegetables. He placed them in his mouth. The food mixed with his saliva when he chewed. The food was unpleasantly hot. He blew on the plate and steam crept off it. He forked one piece of broccoli and blew steam off it. He ate it. He ate his meal. He stood up, picked up what he had on the table. The thin napkin stuck kind of to the table, and he ripped it off, and a scrap of the paper napkin remained caught to the sticky surface. He balled the napkin up on top the greasy plastic plate, and put his fork on top of that, and went to the nearest garbage to throw it all away. He turned away from the garbage. He rubbed his hands together. Mall light filtered through his smeary glasses. He walked out to the parking lot. The day was warm and blue. He felt unsatisfied. He didn't think about it. He found his car, got in, drove home. His apartment was on the second floor of a building that faced a faded road and some grass. He parked along the road. He went upstairs. He walked to the chair in the living room and sat down. He took his glasses off and looked at them. He thought he felt hungry, and was angry, but the feeling departed. He untucked his shirt and wiped his glasses on the fabric. He put them on his face. He took them off again. He wiped them on the shirt's fabric again more vigorously. He was sitting next to a pile of books on one side of the dumpy chair and a plant on the other side. The carpet wasn't always clean. He put his glasses on again. He looked at the wallpaper through his glasses. He leaned back in his chair. He heard a car drive by outside. He heard a child cry downstairs. He leaned over the side of the chair and touched a book. He looked at it, didn't pick it up. He shuffled his weight tiredly around the seat. He yawned. He blinked. The telephone rang. He started slightly. His leg twitched. The phone rang. He leaned over his legs and untied his shoes, took them off his feet. One of his insoles came out; he left it askew on the carpet. He stood up and went to the phone. The phone was on the kitchen counter next to a basket of mail. He sat down on a stool by the phone. It rang. He looked at it. He picked up the receiver, and yawned, and put it near his head. "Good afternoon, Burning speaking," he said. There was a moment of stilted breath. "Oh, you sound weird on the phone," said a voice. Burning leaned forward, legs swung. "Who is this?" he asked. "Um," said the voice. Burning rubbed his neck. "Vowel," said the voice. "Vowel my student," said Burning. "Yeah," said Vowel. Burning kept the phone pressed to the side of his head. He looked out the kitchen window. The sun made the sky white. "Is this illegal— should I hang up?" asked Vowel. "Uh, what do you need?" asked Burning. "Mr. Church?" asked Vowel. "Yes?" said Burning. "Why do you teach?" asked Vowel. "How did you get my number?" asked Burning. He looked at the basket of mail. He reached out and picked up the closest envelope. "The phone book," said Vowel. "Oh," said Burning, "I didn't realize I was listed." He set the envelope back dismissively. "Have you ever heard of something called a god-shaped hole?" asked Vowel. "Are you on a cell phone? I can't hear you that well," said Burning. He turned the receiver away from his mouth and coughed into his fist. His mouth tasted like the mall food. He ran his tongue across the back of his teeth. "I called to see if you were really mad at me," said Vowel. "Why would I be mad at you?" asked Burning. There was a garbled pause. "Do you think I'm going to kill myself?" asked Vowel. Burning rubbed his ear. "I don't think I said that," he said. "What do you think then?" asked Vowel. "Please insert twenty-five cents for the next three minutes," a drowsy female voice said. "Is that a pay phone?" asked Burning. He heard muffled breathing. "I know you think I'm a good writer," said Vowel finally. "Okay," said Burning. The line went dead. Burning heard nothing. He held the receiver to his face, then put it back. He sat blankly on the stool at the kitchen counter. The sun warmed the counter and the floor. He felt hungry again. He went back to the other room and sat there.

Sunday

The supermarket was closed. He stood outside in the parking lot. He felt embarrassed: he came too late. The parking lot was mostly empty. He looked at his car and at the few other remaining cars. He looked at the closed and locked doors of the supermarket, the darkness beyond. He felt hungry. He went back to his car and got in. He sat for a while. The sky he saw through his windshield looked unreliable, maybe rainy. He put his hands on the wheel of the car. He closed his eyes. He opened his eyes and put the keys in the ignition. The car started. He turned on his headlights. He felt unresolved. He drove out of the parking lot and away from the supermarket. He drove by fast food restaurants but didn't stop. He drove by brutal-looking buildings, stores surrounded by characterless parking lots, ugly signs around the hanging telephone wire. He drove away from there, and into a neighborhood of dingy houses, and through it. He was driving away from town and into the country. The road then had farmland on both sides, brown fields expanding emptily under the shady sky. He forgot he felt hungry. He didn't feel anything recognizable. He watched the land lazily and he drove. He went through the farmland and came to a stretch of swampy woods. He thought this must be the place the police look first if a young woman goes missing. He thought it doesn't happen often, but when it does they search the swamp for a body. He could only remember three missing women, but he knew their full names, and remembered details of how they were looked for, even though they were never found and none of the cases were ever solved. When each woman went missing, and especially after she stayed unfound for a long time, many concluded she was killed craftily by a man. The police weren't used to likely murders.

Maybe, he thought, the three of them just went away without a word to anyone, but that wasn't probable. He looked into the swamp moving by. All three girls were named Lucy, he remembered. He kept driving. Presently he saw a windowless building ahead. He slowed the car down. The building was unpainted and had a gravel lot in front of it. There was a handmade sign stuck in the mud by the roadside. The sign said *The Swamp*. Burning stopped driving altogether. He looked at the building. A rain droplet fell onto his windshield and trickled downward. He was holding the steering wheel, but he wasn't driving, he was looking at the building. Two rusty trucks were parked on the gravel lot. He drove again, into the gravel lot, and parked next to the trucks. He didn't know why he was doing this. He opened the car door. The air was heavily warm. He got out of the car, and closed the car door behind him, walking to the entrance of the building. The building's door was old and scraped; there wasn't a knob so Burning reached his fingers into the hole where one should have been. The room inside was dark. He heard radio music. He saw the floor was dirt. At the end of the room was a plywood bar with a shelf of bottles behind it. The only other thing besides was a ratty pool table with a leg missing. A man stood behind the bar, next to a lamp, with a book clenched in his hands. Somebody else in a plaid shirt sat fatly on one of the stools. That was it. Neither of the two turned to notice Burning when he came in. He stopped moving, unsure of what he was doing. He wondered about ordering a drink. He didn't usually drink hard alcohol. He went up to the bar, up to a stool at the end of it. "Don't sit there," said the bartender. Burning looked at him. He was still reading the book. He said, "That stool's funny. It'll tip you." Burning said, "Oh," and moved away. He sat down on a stool one seat removed from the other resident of the bar. He looked at the bartender. "What are you reading?" he asked. "Book about the body without organs," said the bartender, shutting it. He set the book down under the bar. "Warm Pabst is the only beer left," he said. Burning thought. "I'd like a gin and tonic, please," he said. The bartender grabbed around under the bar and produced a mostly empty bottle. "A suggestion of tonic," he said. He set the bottle down on the bar and turned around looking on the shelf for gin. The patron next to Burning glared at him sideways. She was a bloated, fierce-looking woman. Her plaid shirt was halfway unbuttoned. "You know what this is?" she asked. Burning blushed slightly. "Um, no," he said, "what?" The woman grinned widely. "It's a birthday party!" she cried. "Can it, Velma, he doesn't want none of your shit," said the bartender. The woman shook her thick head at Burning. "Excuse him for being a grouch. He's a little brought down since the Department of Health says it's finally putting a stop to this depravity," she said. "I'm sorry to hear," said Burning. "The last birthday party on the planet earth," she said. The bartender put a foggy glass in front of him; he poured the sip of tonic water and then the gin in it. The woman held a drink in her hand. She waved it in front of her. "The past deforms us. The present doesn't exist, it's really just the past's future. And the future—?" she said. Burning leaned around toward her. "I'm sorry?" he said. "You sure are sorry, aren't you? I'm not sorry. You're sorry. Be sorry enough for everyone," she said. Burning picked up his drink. "He'll give you that for an apologia," said the woman. "I don't know why I came in here," said Burning. "You were drawn by the end," she told him. Burning looked at the glass he held. The woman reached over and clinked hers against it. "Here's to failure," she said. "I don't want to drink to that," said Burning. "You will," she said. She winked and gulped down what she had. She looked at her empty glass. "Always kill your babies!" she laughed. Burning set his drink on the bar. "Who are you?" the woman asked him. "Um," said Burning, "I'm a high school teacher." "Who are you?" she asked. "I guess I don't understand the question," said Burning. "Have you ever been so in love . . . ?" said the woman. She frowned suspiciously. "I guess I don't understand that very well either," said Burning. She nodded. "We can never tell anything for sure and because of that we're full of trouble," she said. The bartender grabbed a bottle of whiskey and poured her another drink. "He won't give me the bottle. Not even in the last gasp," she laughed. Her spit landed on the bar. Burning smiled; he picked up his drink and tasted it. "We have to . . . maintain pretenses. Even now," said the woman solemnly. A new song began on the radio. The woman held her drink close to her, her eyes milky. "You know, we used to be *little girls*," she said. "How did we get to be so fucked? It must happen imperceptibly over time. And then all of a sudden! You're going down with the ship!" "Are you going down with the ship?" asked Burning. "We're *always* going down with the—what I meant, if you please, is that eventually we realize everything's entropic drama. So now what?" said the woman. Burning opened his mouth. "That's right!" the woman shrieked. "You're completely right on this one, friend! We either stand the heat or get out of the kitchen. Funny that old turn of phrase is so apt. That's very insightful of you, mister." She drew air in, glared at Burning. "What do you live for?" she demanded. He thought. "I guess I don't ask myself stupid questions," he said. He sipped his drink and winced. The woman pounded the plywood bar fitfully and spilt whiskey on herself. "I'll be damned if you aren't the stranger that wanders into the story at the last minute with all the answers," she cried. Burning looked at the bartender leaning against the shelf. "How do you feel about this?" he asked. The bartender appeared calm. "I think it's an interesting discovery," he said. "Always look on the bright side. It's always darkest before the dawn. Every cloud has a silver lining. Pink sky in the morning, sailors take warning. Why buy the cow when you can get the milk for free? You can't teach an old dog new tricks. You can lead a horse to water, but you can't make him drink. Teachers who can't teach teach gym. Fool me once shame on you, fool me twice shame on me. One good turn deserves another. A stitch in time saves nine. Two tears in a bucket, motherfuck it. Great minds think alike. An apple a day keeps the doctor away. All work and no play makes Jack a dull boy. Time flies when you're having fun. All good boys deserve favor. Children should be seen and not heard. No child left behind. No stone left unturned. A rolling stone gathers no moss. The early bird gets the worm. A penny saved is a penny earned. Absence makes the heart grow fonder. Treat others how you want to be treated. To thine own self be true. If you meet the Buddha on the road, kill him. When it rains, it pours. It's not over until the fat lady sings," said the woman. Burning felt drunk. "What do I owe you?" he asked the bartender. "Always consider the circumstances," the bartender answered. Burning looked at him. He looked at the woman swallowing her drink and wanting more. He bowed graciously, stood up. "That's all folks!" the woman cried and laughed. Burning walked out of the bar; it was raining gently. The sky was dully gray.

NOBODY UNDERSTANDS
THORNY WHEN

I. The News

Thorny When was a little boy, his mother thinks. Her proof is a shoebox of glossy little photographs. The investigators who studied the pictures found the moments of her boy's childhood she chose to capture lacking significant design. She was told her proof meant nothing, couldn't help. She has almost come to understand this. She can't remember being there in the moments she used the camera; she knows those moments don't belong to her—she only owns the pictures. The pictures are evidence that she had a son. Thorny, prettily plump, sat in front of a birthday cake surrounded by girls in Sunday dresses, and he nakedly splashed around in the creek at the edge of the yard, and he grinned holding a wrapped present in front of the Christmas tree, but that doesn't mean much to anybody. She looks at the pictures like artifacts and has almost come to understand that the only confirmation they provide is that her son was little. And that could be said of anybody, she thinks. It doesn't mean anything now, she thinks; but she keeps the shoebox. Even if she's failed to find resonance in what she has left, she still makes herself look at the pictures and never tells her husband she knows their son is dead.

The first video footage available to air on the news channels comes from cameras hastily installed at the edge of the parking lot facing the rear entrance of the police station. An unmarked car arrives and idles; a serious man without a jacket steps unceremoniously out of the passenger-side, walks around, and opens the back door unseen by the camera. Then he is visible escorting two boys toward the station's door. Momentarily the smaller boy turns and smiles, but the man places a hand on the back of his neck and they disappear inside. The clip repeats in obsessive loops on every station as newscasters narrate the importance of the day's events.

Thorny When is found. His parents, Jacob and Kimberly, have not been filmed for television in three years. When Jacob receives a phone call at his office from the chief of police he angrily hangs up suspecting an untimely prank. An officer is dispatched to physically retrieve him. The sun is shining. Jacob sits in the back of a police car driving to the station where he is told he will meet his wife. "And him?" he asks the officer. "He is going to be there?" Jacob is nearly senseless with anticipation or something like dread. The officer is distracted by euphoria. "Miracles really can happen," he tells Jacob. When Jacob and Kimberly arrive separately at the station, a news conference is already being held nearby.

Timmy Victim is herded onto his mark in front of a line of cameras in a featureless room of Town Hall. His family is allowed to lovingly crowd around him. Producers watch from outside the shot as mother, father, and older sister swarm around the child. All arms reach out to him, grabbing his hair and stroking his smiling face.

Timmy's mother wails unintelligibly. The teenage sister

buries her annoyance at being told to remove her faux-gothic makeup; she contrives a warm smile and maintains a hold on Timmy's thin little arm. Timmy's father chants, "Everything is all right now. Everything is going to be fine." This scene plays live with the disembodied commentary of anchormen. "What we're seeing right now, a really heartwarming sight, is Timmy Victim being reunited with his family after a terrible ordeal. Seven-year-old Timmy was kidnapped from his home in White Dog four days ago. A hunt for the boy ended early this morning with the arrest of Normal Chapter, a Buffalo resident. We've been following this story and it's just so gratifying that we're able to report his safe recovery. What makes today especially happy is that, along with Timmy, another boy from White Dog who has been missing for four whole years was found by the police. That child, Thorny When, is now fifteen. We're told the When family is together right now at the White Dog police station having what must undoubtedly be an extremely emotional reunion. Stay tuned for a press conference with that lucky family, but right now let's watch as events unfold at City Hall with Timmy Victim."

The mayor, accompanied by the chief of police, belatedly rushes into the room; his eyelashes flutter and he is awash in the startling light of flashbulbs as photographers scuttle around. "This is a happy day in White Dog!" he declares. He shakes the parents' hands, caresses Timmy's face, and turns to the cameras. "I am so pleased," he says, "at the hard work of our local law enforcement in bringing Timmy safely home today!" The chief of police nods and clears his throat. He says, "This is going to be a message—to *anyone* who ever thinks about hurting a child of White Dog. We will find you and swiftly bring you to justice!" He watches with amusement as journalists copy his speech. "It was awful!" Timmy's mother

interjects. "I couldn't sleep. I couldn't eat. I couldn't imagine
. . ." Her mouth still moves, but she can't continue. "We're
just so very thankful to have him back," says Timmy's father.
"We're headed straight home after this to play some catch."
Timmy remains silent, as instructed, but grins athletically. He
is delighted to be special; right now, surrounded by lights and
cameras, he wants the attention to be undying and has no ex-
pectation that his sudden celebrity will immediately dissolve.

Jacob and Kimberly sit in plastic chairs against the wall.
They look eroded in the blinking fluorescent light. They do
not touch; they do not look at each other. "Well," says Jacob. "How do you feel?" asks Kimberly. Jacob gasps reflexively.
"I'm so happy, I don't know," he says. "How are we supposed
to feel?" she asks. Jacob studies the wall. "I can't keep waiting
like this," he says. "You've always been so good at it," she says.
"What?" he asks. Kimberly doesn't respond. "I'm so thirsty,"
says Jacob. "Officer, uh," says Kimberly, "what's-his-name
promised us water." "Should I go find him? Or find water?" Jacob asks. Kimberly twitches. "No," she says. "He might come
when you're gone." "Who?" asks Jacob. Kimberly watches the
brown door on the other side of the room.

The new footage is of the mostly empty gymnasium of the
junior high school. An art teacher hurries around followed
by a few students; they hang balloons, streamers, and hastily
painted banners that read, majuscule, *WELCOME HOME
THORNY!* and *MIRACLES DO HAPPEN!* as the media
makes final preparations. "We are minutes away from hearing
from Thorny When and his family," a friendly voice assures.
"That name again is Thorny When."

Three chairs and a podium are placed in front of the cameras. Presently an order for silence is given and everybody in the gymnasium watches eagerly as the When family enters accompanied by a police officer and a producer. They are shown to their marks. Jacob stands behind the podium and pulls a leaf of paper from the pocket of his jeans. He looks grim, worry-worn, and avoids smiling to conceal one of his missing yellow front teeth. Kimberly sits seriously next to her son, staring at the floor in front of the congregation of cameras, crying tears slightly stained with eyeliner. Thorny is reticent; he looks almost guilty, but that is too simple. The first images of the boy are featured simultaneously on every news station. He is enduringly scrawny, dressed casually in a baggy sweatsuit, with shaggy black hair and a silver ring through his plump lower lip. He is complicatedly beautiful; his nervously blue eyes betray a depth atypical of his age. The cameras anchor on his visage, only regretfully panning away when Jacob knocks his fist weakly on the podium, coughs asthmatically, and begins speaking.

"Um, when our son was taken from us four years ago," Jacob says, "it was like a part of us was destroyed. It is the hardest thing in the world for a parent to lose a child. The—the experience that came then, with all the media, and the police investigation, and the false leads, and the television appearances we made, and all the efforts to get Thorny back as soon as we could, even as time went on and they told us the chances were so slim we'd get him back, that we should believe he was dead . . . all of that was so overwhelming and we were just so, we were in shock, everything had been turned upside down. But Kimberly and I never gave up hope. Even when they told us he was lost, we put all the money we had in the world into the Thorny When Foundation—which has become our life and continues to do real good for parents in the same boat as us. If I could get one thing across here today, it's that we don't live in the world we grew up in. That would be my message to parents. Listen—there are bad people out there, very bad . . . predators, evil men. Children cannot be let outside without supervision anymore. It's a changed world. I hate to say it. It's true. We have been missing our son for four years and now our family is whole again. It really is a miracle. It's such a wondrous thing. We don't even know what to do. We haven't had much time alone together yet, but at the police station we had a time, uh, we sat around and Kim and me would ask him—do you remember this? Something from when we were together. Do you remember *this*? And he would say, 'Yes!' and my heart . . . would swell. It's been hard for so long. We'll rebuild. My god—nobody should give up hope. There's still a whole darn lot of miracles in this world! This is proof."

As the journalists applaud, Jacob awkwardly grabs his wife and pulls her out of her seat. She leans acquiescently into his bulk, deciding how to react appropriately. "Did I miss anything?" Jacob asks. She smiles goofily and blurts, "We just have a lot of catching up to," swallows dryly, "do!" Both of them turn and gaze at Thorny, hunched over and basically unreadable. The cameras return to his face and remain planted there. His unspeaking image is provided to a national audience, but this obsessive portrait fails to address the profoundest problem implicit in the reunion. Unanswered, the question is at least posed by a chorus of anchormen and journalists too polite to confront the family about it directly. "Why is it—how is it—that Thorny When remained for four long years with his captor, with a man named Normal Chapter?"

The paperwork has been filed. Jacob drives his family home.

Intolerant of silence during this ride, Kimberly struggles for anything to say and finally remembers an important detail. "Your bedroom is exactly the same as always. We kept it the same," she tells her son. Thorny, leaning against the backseat window, thinks about this. "Pokémon bedspread?" he asks. Kimberly smiles, "We can get you new sheets if that's not *cool* anymore." Jacob interrupts, "You used to love that Pokémon so much. All the cards, and video games, and little animation monsters. And that song you used to sing all the time. All the time! Your voice teacher used to tell you you had to *practice* first before you could sing the Pokémon but you were always singing the Pokémon. So nice too. Such a nice voice. How did it go?" Thorny sighs, "I don't remember." "What?" asks Jacob. "How can you not remember? You used to sing it all the time!" Kimberly frowns at him, "Don't push him right now." Jacob stammers, embarrassed. "I'm sorry Thorny," he says. "I don't sing anymore," says Thorny. "Oh," says Jacob. Thorny presses his face against the window. "Pokémon is stupid anyway; and it's for kids," he says. "I, uh, I didn't mean to upset you," Jacob replies. He brakes at an intersection a few blocks away from the house. Thorny stiffens with recognition. As the car drives on, the boy turns around and stares at the spot through the rear window. That specific intersection is his last memory of White Dog; it was where he met Normal Chapter. Kimberly leans around her seat and inspects her son. "We're almost home," she says. Thorny doesn't speak.

II. A Birthday Party

Thorny When had qualities of inchoate beauty that went unrecognized by all except the most sensitive. He was like the other boys eleven years old, but there was a faintly perceptible peculiarity innate in him that was occasionally demonstrated by a stunning expression, mature affectation, or singular gesture. The quality his parents and teachers were most willing to cultivate in him was his gorgeous singing voice. He made friends with children at school, but often avoided them when classes were dismissed. He preferred to wander around his immediate neighborhood alone, climbing trees and lingering under street signs. He was wandering along the road singing an aria to himself when, one unremarkable sunny afternoon, a van pulled up and drove slowly beside him.

Thorny became aware of the van following him and quit singing as he cautiously turned toward it. It was large and white and left him in its shadow; and it seemed framed by the brightness of the sky. He squinted and saw the window was rolled down. A voice came from inside, "Please keep singing!" Thorny was confused; he felt unprepared to respond to such an unfamiliar incident. Unsure, the boy acquiesced and resumed the aria. The van slowed to a halt and Thorny stood in its shadow until he was finished singing. He gazed up at the van's open window and heard applause. "Wonderful!" the voice said, and finally a giant, round head materialized in Thorny's view. He did not recognize the man, but considered he might be somebody who worked with his father. "Thank you," he said. The smiling head disappeared for a moment from the window and the passenger-side door creaked open. The man was leaning over the front seat of the van, inspecting Thorny. "Do you like to sing?" he asked. "Yes," Thorny replied. "Do you know who I am?" he asked. "I'm not sure," Thorny replied. "It's okay. I know who *you* are. You have special gifts," he said. "Everybody at school talks about them." Thorny tried to think about that. "Do they?" he asked. "You bet! They're so jealous," said the man. Thorny smiled at that. "My name's Normal, in case you forgot," said the man. "Hi," said Thorny. "Nice to see you again . . . Paul," said Normal. "Hey, that's not my name!" said Thorny. "Of course it's not! It's Stephen," Normal teased. "It's not Stephen either!" said Thorny. "What, did you change it?" asked Normal. "No! It's *always* been Thorny When," insisted Thorny. Normal grinned, "I know, I know—I was just pulling your chain." He straightened up in his seat and slapped the steering wheel. "Where are you going today then, Thorny?" he asked. "I have to go home and practice for chorus," the boy replied. "You want a ride?" asked Normal. "It's not too far," said Thorny. "A short ride!" replied Normal.

Thorny didn't know why he trusted Normal. It was because the man had chosen him. Normal had recognized what was latent in the boy that nobody else before could see. "You *are* special," he told Thorny. "There is something very special about you. It's your birthday. Do you understand?" Thorny frowned, "But it isn't my birthday!" "But it is!" Normal said. "How?" asked the boy. "It just is," Normal said. "Understand?" "Maybe," said Thorny. "We're going to a party," said Normal. "I thought you were driving me home," argued Thorny. "We're going to *your* birthday party, okay?" replied Normal. "I know it's complicated, but I wouldn't lie to you. Try to understand." Thorny was silent as he watched the familiar streets of his neighborhood pass by. "I think I understand," he concluded. "Understand what?" asked Normal. "It's my birthday," said the boy. Normal was satisfied. "Happy birthday!" he said. Thorny felt unreasonably calm; the two-hour drive from White Dog to Buffalo didn't feel long at all.

Thorny began to nap and his little body serenely slid across the seat of the van until his head was resting on Normal's leg. The sky turned gray before dusk. Normal felt a change know-

ing he was finally actualized. He parked in the gravel drive-
way of a squat house covered in green shingles. When Thorny
awoke he heard the faint noise of the highway just beyond
the rows of ugly homes. "We're here!" Normal told the boy.
Thorny yawned and sat up; he peered out of the window as
Normal leaned over his body and pushed the passenger-side
door open wide. "Is this where my party is?" asked Thorny.
Normal led him into the house with his giant hands covering
the boy's eyes. Thorny giggled; when his face was uncovered
he was surprised by an elaborately decorated room filled with
wrapped presents. Varicolored streamers hung abundantly
and balloons crowded the ceiling. Displayed on a short table
was a pretty pink cake. "Oh wow!" Thorny said. "This is all for
you," Normal told him.

III. The Answer

He sits expressionless in the drab room handcuffed to a metal
chair pulled up so close to the table that its edge pushes into
his large stomach. He is wearing a prison uniform and sitting next to a tired-looking man acting as his attorney. Both
of them stare blankly at the dirty yellow wall. "I'm doing all
right," he says. His attorney checks his watch. Presently a man
walks in, letting the door shut loudly behind him, and sits
down opposite them. His metal chair scrapes against floor. He
drops a thick dossier on the table, opens it, and indiscrimi-
nately flips through it without looking up. Normal wonders
casually if the man is a detective or a psychologist. He cannot
always tell the difference and they don't always identify themselves. When they ask him a question somebody has already
asked him and he says so, they become frustrated and make
him answer anyway. He doesn't care; he has promised complete cooperation because it doesn't make a difference, and

this way he is able to talk about everything again and again. The man looks up from the dossier and asks a question. "I was already asked that question," Normal replies. The man grimaces. "Are we going to have a problem?" he asks. "No," says Normal. "I just thought you'd like to know." He answers the question.

"He was so happy after he opened all his presents up. I gave him everything he wanted—things his unkind parents never gave. He wasn't distracted, he was absorbed; it was his birthday party. I told him every day was his birthday. At the end I brought out a bike with a big bow on it. He really liked that. I told him he could go anywhere, do anything—because he was with me now and I understood him unlike anyone else. And I did. I did love and understand him right from when I first saw him. I wouldn't have taken anyone else. It had to be him, and it was—" The man interrupts him saying, "But when he wanted to go *home*." Normal continues, "Of course he wanted to go home. He wanted to go home. He knew he had to go back home, that his parents would be mad if he wasn't home by bedtime; they would punish him. He was so bright, he knew that, and he asked to go home. I told him we had lost track of time and it was too late for him to go home that day. I had to go to work at the vet in the morning, I said, and would be too tired for the long drive to White Dog and back. He was scared at what would happen to him with his parents, how they would punish him for disobeying. I told him I knew just what to do and pretended to call his house in front of him and talk to his dad. That's why he knew it was okay to stay the first night. I let him sleep in my bed; I slept on the couch in the living room. In the morning I made us a nice big breakfast before I went to work and told him he had to stay in the house but that he could play all day and watch TV. That was Saturday. He didn't mind, he was so happy—that's how I knew he would stay."

"He never offered resistance?" the man asks. Normal considers this. He says, "In the beginning . . . in the beginning. In the first few weeks there was some trouble. He didn't right away understand how easy staying with me and starting a new life would be. I had to hold him down. I had to hold him, and sort of pet him, and tell him, let him know over and over, how special he was, how absolutely special unlike anyone else he was. I asked him if his mom and dad ever told him so. 'Not like that!' he said. Wow. Not like that. Well, I had to hold him. He cried. He was anxious sometimes. I had to be stern in the beginning—just to make sure. I told him he could never go home. His parents would never let him back now. But that didn't matter. It didn't because he was with me now. And, you know, I loved him. I told him so. I loved him and I was the only one who was going to love him the way he needed to be. I worshipped him. Now that he's gone . . ." Normal doesn't say any more and waits for the next question.

IV. A Different Way

When Thorny first rode his new bike around the neighborhood he imagined what would happen if he kept going and went all the way back to his parents. The way would be very long for a bike ride. He would be tired when he reached his old house; his mom and dad would be so angry. When he heard Normal talking to them on the phone sometimes he understood how bad it was. "They say you might as well never come home because they wouldn't let you in anyway," said Normal. "They never really loved you or wanted you. They wanted me to tell you that. They're monsters." When Thorny first heard that he would cry and want to be alone, but he began to realize how lucky it was he was with Normal. Normal really loved him, and wouldn't throw him out like his mom and dad. Normal said, "It only hurts to look back. That's something I learned. We can't be happy that way—we have to move forward, and we're going to, together. I need you." He embraced Thorny and the boy felt better. Both of them felt full of light.

Normal brought home a gray Siamese kitten from his work at the veterinarian's office; he gave it to Thorny as a gift. The boy was ecstatic. Normal watched him play with the animal on the living room carpet. "This is a present for how good you've been so far. I know it's a challenge, but if we stay together we'll always be happy. You are so well behaved and understanding, Thorny. You're perfect, I want you to know that, and I would give you anything you want," Normal told him. Thorny named the kitten Pilgrim.

Normal knew he had finally done something right. He had found his confidence and brought love and beauty into his life. Now he had a purpose, he wasn't just trying to get by. "Something's come over you," a coworker told him. "What?" he asked proudly. "I don't know exactly," she said. "You just don't seem so adrift, I guess. Does that make sense? Not to say you were ever *adrift*, but . . . well, you seem on top of things lately. I'm glad for you. We have to find our happiness in life, you know. What's the secret? Is that kitten you adopted what did it—or you have a girlfriend finally?" Normal smiled. "Everybody has his own secret to success," he said.

Normal watched Thorny at play and was almost overwhelmed by the possibilities of their love. He had an unfulfilled passion that he painfully wished he could introduce uncomplicatedly into the relationship. He didn't know what to do, whether to be delicate or forceful, eventual or immediate. He was convinced this hunger was somewhere inside the boy as well, but didn't know how to reach it. He bent over the boy as he played a video game in front of the television and touched the boy's soft knee as he watched the screen. "Hey, look out! I'm trying to win!" said Thorny. "I just want to be close," said Normal. "Well you're going to distract me!" replied Thorny. Normal watched on silently. "Oh! See? Game over," sighed Thorny, collapsing disappointedly into Normal's bulk. "Do you want to try something different tonight?" asked Normal. "What?" said Thorny. "How about we have a slumber party?" asked Normal. "Just the two of us?" said Thorny.

One day Normal purloined a bottle of ketamine from the locker of anesthetics kept by the veterinarian. He brought it home and poured it in a glass of water for Thorny to drink. "Do you trust me?" he asked the boy, bringing the cup. "Yes," said Thorny. He looked at the cup, suspecting its significance. "You understand everything I do is for us," Normal said. Thorny said, "Of course!" "And so do you know what day it is?" Normal asked. Thorny giggled, "It's my birthday!" "That's right," Normal said, "and to celebrate I have a very important present." He held the cup out. "This is going to show you how much I really do care about you and love you," he said. "What is it?" asked the boy. "Drink it and see. Don't be afraid. This is the only way I can think of to show you," replied Normal. Thorny looked at the cup for a moment. Then he carefully reached out, took it from Normal, and swallowed what was in it.

V. THE FIRST TIME

"The first time, uh—there was a little blood. There was, but he was so calm about it. He was such an angel about it, more than I could have imagined. He was anesthetized, technically, but I wasn't being irresponsible—I just wanted for it to be right, for it to go over well so we could do it again. He wasn't afraid at all, and he just looked at me with those wonderful eyes of his. They were gorgeous; they knew everything. It wasn't sick, it wasn't wrong—it was heavenly perfect. I know it was because I know he understood. Even the first time he did. He kept his eyes open and looked at me all the way through. And I looked back into those beautiful eyes. And we don't regret it. No matter what happens I know we don't regret what that started. It doesn't matter what they might make him say about it because I know how he feels. I believe in god, you know. I do believe in god. I believe I saw god in his eyes every time we made love. I don't know how to explain it, but that's what I saw. And it wasn't much blood. Just the first time, just a little. He wasn't afraid. I told him he wasn't hurt. It was so beautiful. Nobody will take that away from me, how I felt. I cried. My tears and my sweat fell onto his precious body. And—and have I said this before? He said my name. His voice is so beautiful; I hear it all the time. He sang for me. It was exactly like I wanted. It was just the way it should be."

VI. A Happy Family

Kimberly When doesn't remember specific breakfasts because breakfasts are always the same. She doesn't remember the first breakfast after her son disappeared or the first breakfast after she really understood he wasn't missing anymore but gone; she just recognizes that there were breakfasts with him and then those without. She sits in her chair in the living room and tries to remember the breakfast before she first appeared on television, or more recently the breakfast before her son was returned, but can only invoke an unfocused sameness of experience. Thorny still won't appear at the breakfast table now and so at least that nook of the day maintains its foggy smallness about it. It almost comes off like a blessing. Her insignificant morning meals haven't changed even though everything else is so traumatically different. To have a son again, she thinks, is as disturbing to everything she knows as having first believed in his death. It only ever gets harder to live with, whatever happens, from the accrual of it all. This is increasingly impossible to understand the more it needs to be. She thinks, Who is this kid anyway? He is as tall as she would expect a boy his age to be, but otherwise, physically and in personality, wholly unfamiliar. She thinks she once thought she knew what a mother was, but now feels embarrassed by that confidence. In a fantasy of life, the family will make tolerably enough sense. She doesn't really think there is a prayer in actuality.

Kimberly looks at her son, he leaves the room, she closes her eyes and tries to picture him still, meditates on the image, opens her eyes, closes them again, recalls the image again, opens her eyes, and eventually he comes back into the room looking as he did before. She doesn't take any pictures of him. He came back, after four years, with shaggy hair and rings in his face and ears, and he won't talk about it. She doesn't know if she wants him to talk about it. The doctors say it is an eventuality, and that it will help greatly, but that he must be allowed to wait until he is ready. She knows her husband is expectant, if not impatient—not because he is eager to hear the details of something so unknown to the family ordinary that it can only exist to him as a vague idea or rough sketch of experience, but because he anticipates it will result in a change in the boy. She sometimes believes that maybe the unreleased injury he is keeping inside is exactly what prevents him from acclimating with his family again, but she's never sure. She doesn't know what to think.

Jacob knows he is to be understanding, but that he must also be stern. He asks Thorny to remove the jewelry from his lip and from his ears, and then he demands it. "You can't have your picture taken like this," he says. Thorny responds, "I don't want my picture taken!" "You have to," he says. "A professional is coming. It's for the papers. There's no argument." He takes the boy to the mall for a proper haircut. The stylist attempts to talk cheerfully about miscellany, but from where Jacob watches he can see she knows who her customer is. She looks shamefully enticed. When the picture is printed and broadcast on news stations, Thorny is smiling and seems healthy, groomed, and rescued.

Kimberly sits in her chair in the living room and watches her son's portrait appear on the television screen. She is watching a special on the Teller Albert show featuring Timmy Victim and his happy family. Thorny refused the invitation to appear on the show to protest the strict rules his father imposes to ensure his safety. When the producers brought up the possibility of Kimberly and Jacob participating in their son's absence, Thorny suggested he would kill himself if they accepted. "They're just going to talk about us if we're not there to defend ourselves!" Jacob complained. "What do we have to defend?" asked Kimberly. "If we're not *there* then they'll bring up who-knows-what kind of untrue speculations," said Jacob. He claimed he was refusing to watch the special when it aired, but since he is not home Kimberly assumes he is viewing it at his office.

The Victim family emotionally tells host Teller Albert about what a frightening ordeal the kidnapping was and how the few days Timmy was missing felt like years. Teller lets them know how lucky they really are to have him back. She eventually asks the parents, "Did Normal Chapter do anything to your son—did he touch him?" The parents both deliver cautious sighs and shake their heads. The mother says, "No. Thank god, no! Timmy is being very honest with us and tells us he experienced no sexual harm." Teller interrupts, "Do you believe Normal Chapter would have hurt him in that way had he more opportunity?" The father responds, "There is no doubt in my mind. Normal Chapter is a very evil man. He is definitely a pedophile, he is extremely dangerous for children." Teller nods solemnly. She asks, "Do you think Thorny When was sexually abused?" The parents pause gravely. "Yes, Teller," the dad says finally, "we do think he was ritualistically raped." The mother adds, "It's absolutely unbearable to think of!"

Kimberly just watches. Before the media attention around his return, she hadn't heard Thorny's name on television for three years. Now a grinning child being interviewed on television is saying, "I'm glad to god I wasn't so hurt as Thorny When." She stands up during a commercial break, puts on a nightgown despite the early hour, and fixes herself a vodka tonic. When she falls back into her chair, Thorny's picture is on the screen again. It is soon replaced with Normal Chapter's mug shot and images of local street corners. Teller Albert is narrating the story of the boys' recovery. "It was an astute young high school student from White Dog who reported to police that he had recorded the license plate number of a suspicious van he saw the day of Timmy's disappearance. After some sleuthing, local police learned that the vehicle belonged to a resident of Buffalo named Normal Chapter. Authorities were immediately sent to question him at the veterinarian's office where he worked an unskilled position. According to them, the man was hostile, nervous, and highly suspect. A search warrant for his home was obtained in short order. His house was raided and the two boys were recovered and immediately handed over to local police in White Dog. A happy ending for a story that could have ended much worse. A nightmare averted for one innocent child, before it was too late, and a second chance for Thorny When, a boy who mysteriously lived that nightmare every day for so long."

Kimberly swallows most of her drink and the phone rings. She leans over her chair and picks up the receiver. "Are you watching?" she hears her husband ask. "Of course," she sighs. "We could have been there to do damage control," Jacob says. "She would ask us questions we don't know how to answer," she replies. "Not if we were right there in the studio!" says Jacob. "That's how's these things work. You know that by now." She says, "I don't know, I have to go." "Thorny could have said he prayed every day that the police would come rescue him and that he was afraid for his life for four years. Instead there's some smug know-it-all asserting that our son was 'ritualistically' raped!" says Jacob. Kimberly hears Thorny drop something on the floor of his room upstairs. "It's not our fault," she concludes. "I'm going to go now." She drinks her drink again.

At dinner an argument begins over Thorny being restricted from the Internet that illogically leads to the boy demanding his cat back. "You don't have a cat," says Jacob. "Yes I do," Thorny insists. "His name is Pilgrim, and he's a gray Siamese, and I've had him for four years!" Jacob slams his fist on the table. "That's that man's cat!" he screams. "That cat belongs to *him*! It's not coming into our house—our family home!" Thorny runs away from the table and his parents hear glass break as he stomps up the stairs. Kimberly is silent. Jacob breathes heavily. "When is he going to start acting like my son?" he asks.

VII. The Cover Story

"They're looking for me," Thorny said. "They want to get you back because they hate it that everything is so much better for you here," said Normal. "I don't understand, they keep saying I've been kidnapped," said Thorny. "That's a lie they told the police so that I'd get in trouble if you left me," Normal said. "Can't we stop them?" asked Thorny. "We just have to be careful is all, and we'll be fine," said Normal.

Thorny wanted the attention to stop, but his parents wanted to ruin everything. They started a website about him that he would read. What he hated most was how they pretended to be sad; they wrote online about how they dreamt that the family would be complete again. He had been with Normal for two years. His mom and dad were only upset because they couldn't control him. Everything they put on their website was a lie, he realized now. They didn't love him enough, or maybe at all, even before he found Normal. He wanted everybody reading their website to realize he couldn't go back. One day he left a message on their website's guestbook, signing it with Normal's surname. He wrote, *How much longer are you going to look for your son?* They should have given up. They should have listened to anyone who said their son was dead. That's what Thorny wished would happen.

The story was that Thorny lived with his father, a widower, and was educated at home. He spent most of his time with Normal, but when he was at work Thorny played video games, or watched television, or used the Internet. He met a few boys from the neighborhood and was allowed to spend time with them. "Just watch what you say," said Normal. "Do you understand?" Thorny said, "Yes." "I want to protect you," Normal told him. The boy accepted invitations to spend the night at the houses of friends, but he never much enjoyed it. Some kids helped him discover pornography and prank phone calls. When he was fourteen he went with a girl he met at the mall to her junior high school prom. "How was it?" Normal asked when he returned home amusingly dressed in a rented tuxedo. "Okay, I guess," he said. "I'm glad I don't have to go to school." That summer the police brought him home four different times for staying out past a curfew for minors. Normal affected a frown and said, "Go to your room, kid." Thorny bowed his head and disappeared into the bedroom they shared. Normal smiled at the police officer and said, "Thanks a lot—that boy is a handful sometimes!"

As he grew, Thorny developed an unwelcome tendency to tease Normal about certain aspects of their relationship. This would encourage an argument between them that could be long and exhausting, but it was always resolved eventually; as an apology, Normal drove the boy to the mall to shop for clothes. When Thorny became desirous of a few piercings, Normal initially disallowed it but was persuaded through the boy's nagging to consent. He drove Thorny to a little shop and said, "He's old enough. I wish he didn't want to grow up so fast, but I try to give him whatever he wants. Anyway, it is his birthday."

Normal and Thorny lay together in bed, facing each other with bodies under covers. A strand of moonlight fell softly across the room. "What were you like when you were my age?" asked Thorny. Normal watched the boy's face. "I wasn't anything until I met you," he said. "But how did you feel?" insisted Thorny. Normal thought silently then said, "Everything was awkward. My mother was terrible. That's all there was— my mother, and younger brother, and me. I couldn't do anything right, I guess. But my mom made me feel that, I realize that now. She didn't know how to raise boys at all. My brother wanted to go to school, but she made him join the army, and he's dead now. She thought I was nothing and raised me as nothing. I spent so many years not knowing what to do with myself. Years having to put up with the way that she didn't know how to treat anybody in the house. Some people just shouldn't be around children. She always told me I was a useless brute when I was a kid, and I thought I must have been, so I didn't advance myself at all. I really did believe all the horrible things she made me feel about myself until I realized life wasn't going to change unless I did something. I think you saved my life in that way especially. I wasn't going anywhere. You showed me I could do something beautiful. And now I can always be happy." "That's really nice," said Thorny, eyes closed. He felt so special he didn't expect Normal would ever want another boy.

VIII. A Prayer

Thorny won't listen and bow his head. "We're saying grace— right now," his father repeats. Thorny stares at him unresponsively. Kimberly waits with her hands folded; she wants to remain uninvolved. Things like this shouldn't be so hard. "Thorny, we're going to pray now. This is what we do as a family before dinner. We're not going to touch any of this food your mother worked so hard to cook until you cut out the tough guy act and do this with us," says Jacob. A nearly unbearable pause follows. Finally, Kimberly sighs and urges,

"Please, Thorny, just so we can eat." Jacob flinches angrily. "No, *not* just so we can eat," he says. "We are saying grace because we are genuinely, deeply thankful that the lord has blessed us with the safe return of our only son after four years! *That* is why we're going to pray. And Thorny! You can act like an ingrate toward me—but you'll regret you ever acted that way to god!" Kimberly listens to the sound of the refrigerator. "Maybe we shouldn't provoke him," she murmurs. "I'm not provoking *anyone!*" yells Jacob. "I'm telling our son that if he doesn't start changing his *attitude,* he knows where the *door* is!" Blushing with anger he leans toward Thorny, waving a fork exaggeratedly. "We do so much for you! So much! We gave up everything to find you! For so long! We both gave up our *jobs,* our *salaries,* so that we could dedicate more time to working to find our son, our beautiful, obedient eleven-year-old child, against all odds, because usually when a kid goes missing that long he's probably *dead!* All our money and our time and our energy we invested in your return—and now what? Now it's been months and we don't have our son back! We sure have his body! We have his needs! 'I want this, I want that!' We have his bad behavior and his unwillingness to talk to anyone, not even the doctors that know how to help! But where is that boy who left us? I don't know you. I don't know why you are making it so *difficult* for all of us! We want to help you, we do! Nobody's the enemy here. It's up to you now to start learning how to get along with what you have. Do you hear me, Thorny? Otherwise, I don't know what to say to you!" Thorny doesn't move to look at his disturbed father. Jacob indignantly waits for a response. Finally, the boy's lips move slightly and he whispers, "You didn't find me." "What?" Jacob coughs. Thorny lifts his gaze and says, "You say you gave up everything to find me, but you didn't find me. Nothing you did ever helped to find me. I was found by mistake." Jacob is inarticulate with fury. Thorny continues, "Remember how right after I was brought back here, the news people made a big deal about how somebody using the name Chapter posted a comment on your stupid website asking how long you were really going to keep looking for your son? That was me who wrote that. Maybe you don't know what it was like when we were together before. I do." Jacob stammers as if to speak, but instead throws his weight across the table, reaches out, grabs his son, and shakes his body while plates of food clatter. Kimberly is amazed and can offer no intervention. She watches Thorny's face pale as he is thrown about in his father's grasp. She doesn't know what she is even seeing.

Kimberly is unused to finding the door to Thorny's room ajar. It would seem like a lazy oversight if it weren't so incongruous with his carefully maintained unavailability. Although denied a lock on the door, he always slams it shut. That it is open a little right now is startling enough to imply an invitation. She doesn't want to talk to him, but guiltily decides she has to try. She approaches and glimpses Thorny reposed unmoving on his bed in the dark. "Are you awake?" she whispers. There is no answer. She timidly pushes the door open wider and the hallway light brightens his room. "I'm your mother," she states blankly. She knows he's awake. He's not stopping her yet, so she enters the room. The room that seemed inappropriate to her for most of the time he was gone is now his room again. She looks around and prefers it now that he has removed most reminders of how it used to be. At least somebody living lives here, whoever he is, she thinks. He seems to be waiting for her to do something, perhaps too frightened to offer another gesture. She fumbles and descends upon the extreme edge of his bed.

She tries to know enough here. He's crying. "I haven't been that much of a mother, I guess," she admits. "It's not your fault. I know you can't tell me what that's supposed to mean. I'm sorry if I let you down. The reason is that, even if I'm confused, I know I do love you. I'm sorry I never say that and that I never know what to say to you. I sort of feel like I'm buried underground or something sometimes. I have to do better. I'm going to. Maybe we can promise each other to try harder because what we're doing now isn't working, right? I don't understand your pain or know if I can or want to. I always thought you were dead. Your dad didn't, but he's stubborn. The TV psychics brought us on their shows and told us you were dead almost every time. And they don't usually do that in these cases. The police just stopped talking to us after a while. Now you're here again, but this awful thing has happened, and I don't know how to understand your pain. Is there any way to fix it? Is there something I can do or will you say something? You can say something. Please say something. You can say I'm a bad mother, I know I am. I'm telling you it's okay. I need to hear you now."

Thorny can't stop himself. He looks at her, and understands the generosity of her effort, and he does speak. "Don't say bad things about yourself. I don't want you to feel upset. Maybe if things didn't happen like they did we'd pretend everything was the way it should be, but we wouldn't be happy. And I would make myself believe I loved you because I had to, and that would make things bad too. I'm sorry. Because I don't love you. I don't know you. How can you love somebody you don't know? Do you really love me or are you telling me that because it's what you're supposed to say? Everything is so fucked up, Mom! I don't see how it's ever going to get right again." He almost gasps at himself after the blurt. His room feels unearthly, floating away somewhere. Kimberly begins to cry. She says, "Whatever horrible experiences you've had, Thorny, can be dealt with so you can live a healthy life!" Thorny goes for it, "That's not it! That's not what hurts me so much. I'm not saved. Everything I wanted is gone. I lost what made my life, and I can't get it back ever, and the whole world knows but won't say! I was special! Don't you get it? I was in love! I love somebody I'll never see again."

The room is dizzy. Kimberly is rigid now and unexpressive. When she realizes Thorny is waiting for her to do something, she wheezes, "Say that again." Thorny speaks in a terrified breath, "I love him." Reflexively she pulls back her arm and strikes him. When he doesn't offer resistance, she strikes him again. Her abuse is ungainly and the most honest, startling thing she remembers doing. She falls forward onto him, and in the dim room she begins to bark tears and scream, and she hits him again and again. She croaks and shrieks, but the only intelligible word she repeats is, "Don't!" Thorny doesn't know what happens now. He can't really feel anything but the loss. He is numb and now that he has made the admission he is sort of gone from this. Nothing matters here because he is tormented by a singular question. He wants to know, with the love they had, why Normal had to ruin it all forever.

IX. THE NEW BOY

Normal had said nothing, but he began to detect an absence that became more pronounced with time. There was something wrong that kept him from feeling the same as he had earlier. Thorny was growing up and developing ungainly adult traits—the downy promise of his childhood was becoming muddled by something harder to worship. The boy's sensitivities were advancing, but new awkwardness and temperamental unpredictability now defined him as well. Normal loved Thorny, but cultivated a hunger for the younger sensations provided when he found the undiscovered beauty on the road, knew the child was his solution, and brought their lives together. Undeniably Thorny had to grow—he couldn't ignore or retard that indefinitely, but he started to fantasize a way he could satisfy himself exactly as he needed without destroying the love he already had. He concluded he would be compounding his achievements by refusing to wallow in insecurity and doubt, as he had for most of his life, and engineering a positive change instead.

Thorny awoke one morning to find Normal decorating the living room with many streamers and balloons. "Are we having a party?" he asked. "It's a birthday party," replied Normal. "My birthday party?" he asked. Normal looked down at him from his task. "All of our birthday parties," he said. Thorny was puzzled. "So what's going on, really?" he asked. "Well," said Normal, "I am getting you a present." "Yeah, what is it?" asked Thorny. "I think it is time for you to have a brother," Normal told him. The boy did not agree as Normal had dreamed.

"What do you *mean?*" Thorny cried. He was restless, pacing around the partly decorated room. "I mean," said Normal, standing on a chair unrolling a streamer, "you know what I always say! I mean we can't look backward—we always have to move into the future. I thought that would make you excited. Aren't you excited? It's going to mean a lot for us. We're starting a family." Thorny was churlish and scared. "Did I do something wrong?" he asked. "Thorny, no! Of course not," said Normal. "What are you even getting at asking that?" Thorny replied, "But it's just us!" Normal said, "You're not giving this idea a chance."

When Normal left and returned with a cake, Thorny was in tears. "You're just going to pick up some boy—?" he demanded. "You have to trust my judgment. You'll realize I have a great plan for all of us," Normal said. Thorny followed him into the bedroom where Normal brought several tubes of wrapping paper out of the closet. "I don't think this is a good idea. You can't do this, Normal. I don't know why you want to," said Thorny. "I'll find a brother you'll love," Normal replied. "You won't find anyone who can replace me!" huffed Thorny. He was becoming hysterical. Normal set down the wrapping paper and grabbed the boy, held him tight in his arms. "I don't want to replace you. I never could. I love you," Normal spoke into his hair. "I remember how small you were, made for my hug." Thorny struggled superfluously, allowing himself to remain in the embrace.

The best thing to do was go forward resolutely, Normal thought. It would be a struggle to start, but soon everything would be right. Thorny would realize this. "I need your help," he told him. The boy pouted, didn't respond. "To make this work I'm going to need your support—or else something might go wrong. I don't want anything to go wrong. I want us all to be so happy. Don't you understand?" he asked. "Don't do this!" Thorny replied. "You say that now, but you'll see. I know I can trust you," said Normal. He left in his van and returned with a boy named Timmy Victim. Four days later he was arrested.

The child was frightened and erratic at his birthday party. Normal had to unload him out of the van and carry him yelping into the house. Thorny had been waiting fearfully in the decorated room. "What *is* this?" he asked. "His name is Timmy!" said Normal, struggling to hold the child's tantrum.

"Look, Timmy! It's all for you—your birthday party!" The child was lost in his frenzy, flailing to escape Normal's arms. He tried to motion the child's body toward Thorny. "And this is your new brother!" he said. "Shut up," said Thorny. "Quick, Thorny, sing the birthday song!" said Normal. "I don't want to," said Thorny. "This is a very delicate situation!" Normal pleaded. Thorny scowled, started to sing unenthusiastically. Timmy, still captured in Normal's hug, began to calm down and gaze around the room with wet eyes. His runny face was still contorted in fright, cheeks idiotically burning, but the shrill huff settled in his throat. Normal encouraged him. "These presents are all for you!" he cheered. "See? No reason to be so upset. All your dreams come true here." Timmy gulped, "Ma—Mommy?" "Your mommy told me how good you were, how well behaved," said Normal. "She said to only let you open the presents if you were on your best behavior." He slowly released the child, who was too bewildered to move. Normal had to kind of prop him up. He ran a soothing palm across his downy head. Thorny quit singing and retreated into a corner, offended. "We're going to all get along real well," Normal said, directing Timmy to the presents like a crippled pet.

In the bedroom Normal was offering Thorny caresses that were rebuffed. "Let's both go back out, we can't leave him unsupervised yet," Normal said after a little of that. He doted on Thorny impatiently. His pleading gaze was avoided. "Why did you pick him, Normal? He had to be the first one you saw!" Thorny yelled. "He's going to take some time is all," Normal replied. Thorny threw himself dramatically on the bed. "Get away from me," he said. "Come back into the other room," Normal urged. "No! This is bullshit! Just take him back, please, Normal! Take him back where you found him and everything might still be okay!" the boy screamed into the mattress. "I love you," said Normal. "Do you love *him?*" asked Thorny. "We're all going to love each other," he replied. Thorny didn't respond anymore, it was beyond the worst, and Normal had to leave to monitor the child in the living room. He was playing with a new remote control truck; his lips were covered in chocolate cake. When he saw Normal he said, "I got to go now. My sister will be jealous when she sees my new toys!"

When Normal went to work he gave Timmy a tranquilizer but warned Thorny that he would wake up in the afternoon. They stood over the child as he slept on the couch. "Just be careful," said Normal. "If he gets too much to handle, feed him this pill and it will knock him out again until I'm back. I trust you so much. If anything goes wrong it might be the end of all of this. Do you understand?" Thorny pretended to be preoccupied. When Normal left he watched the new child's unconscious body with contempt. Timmy woke up hours later as Thorny watched television. "I have to go home!" he cried. Thorny said, "You can never go home again." "But I—I want to, to see my mommy and dad!" said Timmy. "Okay," said Thorny, turning around from the television set, "there's one special way for you to go home right now." "How?" asked Timmy. "Eat this pill," said Thorny.

Thorny and Timmy sat in front of the television playing a video game on the second day. "Normal says my parents are really angry," said Timmy. "Shut up," said Thorny. Timmy said, "They don't even want me back they said, but Normal said they didn't mean it. Normal said he was going to fix everything. Do you think I'll get to go home tomorrow? Thorny? Do you think I'll get to go home tomorrow or do you think my parents really are that mad?" Thorny concentrated on the game. "I know my mommy and dad aren't angry really—but I've never been away so long before. At least I got all these cool new toys. I kind of like it here with all this fun stuff. Do you live here? Hey, Thorny—you live here, right?" asked Timmy. "Yes," said Thorny. "Are you Normal's best friend?" asked Timmy. Thorny tossed his controller between his legs. "Listen," he said, "don't get any ideas about Normal, got it? Normal and me live together, and what we have is very special together, and you're not going to replace me because you're a stupid little shit and you even look like one!" Timmy frowned. "You're mean," he said. "I want you to die," replied Thorny, grabbing his controller again. Timmy won the game. "I get to take home *all* my new toys when I go," said Timmy.

Normal parked the van sideways in the yard, jumped out, and burst into the house on the third day. He locked the door behind him. Thorny had trapped Timmy in the kitchen pantry by blocking the door with a chair. Normal heard the new child's muffled cries. "I just want, want to go *home* n—now! I have to go, go to the . . . bathroom! I have to go *home* to see Mommy!" Thorny sat languidly on the kitchen floor lighting matches and watching them burn on the tile. "What happened?" Normal asked. He was sweaty and trembling. "Huh? Oh—he was being a stupid shit again," said Thorny. "Let me out!" Timmy screamed. "But what happened? Did you talk to anyone? Did anyone come to the door?" said Normal, peering out of a window into the backyard. "What are you talking about?" asked Thorny. He stood up. "I didn't know *what* I was going to find here!" said Normal. "What happened?" yelled Thorny. "Some men," said Normal, "uh, with questions. About being in White Dog. They came at work. They must know *something*." "Who? What do they know?" asked Thorny. "I said I was a good citizen, I didn't know anything about it! I must have lent my van to a friend. How could they believe that?" Normal said. "Are we in trouble?" asked Thorny. "I'm not sure," said Normal. "I'm not sure what they know." "You must have done something wrong, Normal!" said Thorny. "I can't think. I don't know," said Normal, spinning, sitting down. "If they're not here now, then they don't know everything— but they were asking questions about the van in White Dog on the day I took the boy." Timmy was silent, having exhausted himself and fallen asleep on the floor of the pantry. "Something's wrong," said Normal. Thorny watched Normal panting and sweating and he began to cry. "This is your fault," he said. He ran toward Normal and beat his fists against his broad chest. "Why did you have to be so stupid? You're going to get caught with this kid you took!" Normal tried to restrain him. "Please, Thorny! It wasn't supposed to be this way. It was all supposed to go right—like it did before, with you!" he said. Thorny didn't calm down. "Get rid of him!" he yelled. "I can't *now*," Normal argued. "Yes! Drive him far away and leave him there. We could move. We could change our names," Thorny said. "Somebody *saw* me," said Normal. "It's the only way," said Thorny. "Let me think about this," said Normal. "If the police know, they'll come! And it will all be over! We have to do something," said Thorny. Normal was too ambushed to hold the boy still as he wailed. Finally he said, "You're right." "We have to get rid of the kid and go," said Thorny. "Okay," said Normal. "When?" asked Thorny. "It will take a few days to get everything ready," Normal said. They were silent.

Timmy was unconscious on the couch in the living room; Thorny and Normal were emptying the bedroom closet, deciding what they needed to take with them. It was a sunny afternoon. "Where's the cat carrier?" asked Thorny as he sorted through his clothes. "What?" said Normal. "The cat carrier for Pilgrim," he said. "I forgot to pick one up at work, Thorny, I'm sorry," Normal replied. He put a shoebox of photographs into a suitcase open on the bed. "What are we going to do?" asked Thorny. "We can carry him in a pillowcase," said Normal. There was a knock on the door. Thorny felt like he was falling.

"We can run," Normal said, grabbing the suitcase. "What's going to happen?" asked Thorny. The police broke the front door open. Everything fell out of the suitcase. Pictures of Thorny suddenly scattered across the floor. Neither of them moved. "I love you," said Thorny. "Let's go!" said Normal. He held out his hand. Men rushed into the bedroom pointing guns. They barked orders, but Normal wasn't listening. Thorny didn't take his hand. The boy stood there and looked into Normal's eyes. He was thinking of his goodbye forever. He opened his mouth, and began to sing, and that was all Normal understood. It was the saddest but most beautiful song Normal had ever heard and it filled him full of light. When his face was on the ground, lying suddenly in pictures of Thorny, and he felt the weight of a gun pressed against his neck, he could still see the boy. Thorny was raised high over the shoulders of several men and Normal could still see him as he was being carried away. And he could hear the song. He could still hear Thorny singing to him even when the boy was out in the yard, being tucked into a police car. Even when Thorny stopped singing, and never sang again, he could hear it.

X. A STATEMENT

"I didn't lie about anything. I answered all the questions the best I could. I want everybody to understand me. Because I'm a good man. Sometimes I make mistakes, but I work hard to understand and to be good. And I started something good. I know, no matter what happens to me for what I've done, at least I tried. I made something beautiful, even if I ruined it, instead of going stupidly through life. I don't know if anybody is going to understand that. Most people think I'm a bad man on principle for what I did. They think I hurt people. That's not what I was trying to do. A bad man is somebody who never tries to do anything great in life. A good man is somebody who looks for beauty. I know I made mistakes. I don't know what punishment I'll get, but I know I deserve punishment for what I've done. But what I mean is I've let love down. I could have had the greatest love forever, but I made a misstep. I failed the boy and ruined his life because my ambition got in the way of my understanding. That's my fault, that's my crime. I could be living so happily in love right now. I saved that boy to give him understanding and intimacy. I mean I thought I could understand him. That would have been perfect love—to understand him in a way nobody else could. But I failed at that. Now there isn't another chance. We can't be together anymore. And it's going to be so hard for him. He's such a complicated, sensitive boy. Where is he going to find the support he needs? It should have been me. It should have been, but even though I thought I understood him, I didn't all the way through. Nobody understands Thorny When. That's what hurts me the most. So I deserve whatever I get. I never meant it to end this way. What I wanted was to be good. Now it's all gone."

THE POKÉMON MOVIE

One road went through Napoleon, a hamlet of meadows and hay fields surrounded by woods and hills; the road was fading into the earth. Ash sat in the quiet living room of his parents' house. None of the lamps were turned on, but the fading afternoon light shone through the windows and created stark shadows in the corners. Sissy was in the bathtub. Thankful sat next to a plastic plant at a table in the dining hall of the American Legion. He tore small pieces from the paper tablecloth. A plate with a cheeseburger on it and a glass of beer were set before him. He was frowning. A woman with dirty hair and a paunch walked up to him and said, "How's the grub?" Thankful didn't look at her. "Haven't touched it," he said. "Want anything else?" asked the woman. Thankful tore a small piece from the paper tablecloth, didn't say anything. An old tank from the Korean War was displayed out in front of the American Legion, in the grass by the road, and a light shone on it at dusk. Thankful parked the car, got out, walked into his house, entered the living room, and saw Ash sitting in one chair and Sissy unmoving on the couch, in the dark. Ash sat with his hands in his lap, his body layered with angular shadows and dim light. Sissy occupied one edge of the couch; she was rigid; she was watching her son. Thankful stopped in the doorway; he looked at his son and then at his wife. Nothing happened. The walls of the living room were decorated with family portraits in cheap frames, and Ash sat in a chair, and Sissy was unmoving on the couch, and Thankful stood still by the doorway, and nothing happened. Then there was a faint, growing noise. Ash walked out of the front door of the house, followed by his dad, and then his mom, all of them already looking to the sky. They stood close together in the yard and listened to the roaring noise growing louder. When the roaring noise grew louder still it seemed to fill up all of the black night sky. The noise was palpable, the family felt their bones shake, but they didn't see anything until presently a vague red light appeared, blinking. The family watched the blinking red light travel through the dark sky, high above the ground, and when it was over their heads a strong wind stung their faces. The light kept moving and all the sensations went away; the noise faded just as it came. Ash, Sissy, and Thankful stood in the yard for a long time, not speaking, still watching the black sky. Finally, Sissy spoke. She said, "A flying saucer." There was silence. Nothing happened. "A helicopter," said Thankful. Ash was crying.

Ash sat in the quiet living room with his parents. Bright sunlight shone through the windows. Nothing happened. Ash sat with his hands folded in his lap. Sissy and Thankful sat on either end of the couch. Thankful had the day's newspaper in his lap but wasn't reading it. Sissy watched her son. Ash was thinking. There was silence and light. "I want to say something I'm afraid to," said Ash. Nothing happened. Sissy was in the kitchen; she closed the stove and walked into the empty living room. Thankful sat in his car in the parking lot of the American Legion. He looked at the tank from the Korean War that was displayed by the road. The tank was old

and heavy; it looked like a decoration and not a weapon that
was once used in combat. It never moved, but a light shone
on it at dusk. An American flag waved on a flagpole and underneath it a Prisoners of War flag waved. Sissy and Thankful
sat in the living room on either side of the couch and bright
sunlight shone through the windows. Ash sat with his hands
in his lap. Nothing happened. Finally, Ash spoke. "I want to
go," he said. Sissy and Thankful didn't move. Then, Thankful
moved; he leaned over the side of the couch and picked up
the day's newspaper from the floor. He put it in his lap. "We
know you do," said Thankful. Sissy watched her son. "I want
to because I have to," said Ash. "You're young," Sissy said.
"It's a lot of responsibility," said Thankful, "and it's not something you're ready for." Nothing happened; there was silence
and light. Finally, Ash spoke. "I just have to," he said. Thankful didn't answer, he opened the newspaper but he didn't start
reading it. "I love you," Ash told his parents. "There are evil
things in the woods," said Thankful, looking at his newspaper
without reading it. "But I want to be the very best, like no
one ever was," said Ash. Thankful looked at his son over the
newspaper and then he looked away and said, "We know you
do." "And I'm ready!" said Ash. "I'm sure I am." Thankful sat
next to a tall plastic plant at a table in the dining hall of the
American Legion with a woman with dirty hair and a paunch.
The woman had a can of beer and a hunting magazine set out
on the table; she was reading the hunting magazine and talking. "When I go hunting it don't bother me," she said, "whatever's in them woods. It's old wives' stories. What's in them
woods but plenty of deer and turkey?" Thankful was looking
at the woman. "There's nothing in the woods but animals and
trees," he said. The woman said, "Just old wives' stories about
the evil, then. Bet that's it." Nothing happened. "What was it

like fighting?" asked the woman. She sipped her can of beer. "It was like being in elementary school," said Thankful. "If I weren't so old I'd like to fight a war," said the woman. "Is there still war?" asked Thankful. "You know it," said the woman. "They let women fight it too. Wars in Iraq and Afghanistan." "Those are counties in Minnesota," said Thankful. The woman said, "You know it." Nothing happened. Sissy turned on the washing machine and walked into the dark living room; at first she couldn't see anything, then she saw nobody there. Sissy was lying on one side of the bed she shared with her husband and Thankful was lying on the other side holding the day's newspaper. "An article here says the mayor wants the road fixed," said Thankful. Sissy did not move and was silent. "It sure needs to be fixed," said Thankful. Sissy stood at the edge of Ash's bed and watched her son sleep, his body layered with angular shadows and dim light. Ash lay in the backyard grass looking at the afternoon sky. His best friend Computer sat nearby. "What am I going to do?" asked Ash. "What are you going to do about what, Ash?" asked Computer. "You know!" said Ash. "About my parents." "They won't per-mit you to do something you want to," said Computer. "They won't let me follow my dreams," said Ash. "What is it like to have dreams?" asked Computer. "It hurts," said Ash. "Why do you want to experience pain?" asked Computer. Ash frowned, sat up. "It's complicated," he told his friend. "Are you going to leave, Ash?" asked Computer. "I don't know," said Ash. "I have to." Computer thought about this. "If you leave, your parents will miss you," he said. "I know," said Ash. "It's hard, but I have to face the challenges." Computer said, "If you leave, I will be alone." Ash heard a car drive away. Thank-ful sat still in the barber's chair, covered with a smock, as the barber stood next to him and snipped at his hair with a pair of shiny scissors. Sunlight shone into the room from the windows and onto the screen of the television that sat on top of a cabinet. There was a motorcycle race on the television, but Thankful could only hear it because of the bright beams of light that shone onto the screen. The barber held his scissors up and sprayed them with a can of disinfectant. Nothing happened. "Think the road's going to get fixed?" asked the barber. The barber turned Thankful around in the chair so he was facing a mirror and Thankful saw himself wrapped in a smock. "Shorter," said Thankful. "Can do," said the barber. Then he said, "If you ask me, I think the road ought to have gotten fixed a long time ago and that we spent all that money on a new football field behind the school instead and that didn't do us any good and the road kept falling apart. Politicians all got rocks in their heads." He snipped at Thankful's hair again and little strands of it began to fall down on the smock and the floor below. "The road's important. We all use that road," said the barber. The barber turned Thankful away from the mirror and Thankful saw the beams of light that shone onto the television on top of the cabinet. There was silence except for the sounds of the motorcycle race and the snipping scissors. Thankful watched short strands of his hair collect in the folds of the smock he was wrapped in. "If Barack Obama gets voted president," said the barber, "then nothing'll get done. It's unbelievable. All the civil servants of Napoleon will sit around all day whistling 'Dixie' if a welfare liberal like Barack Obama gets elected for president." The barber turned Thankful around so he was facing the mirror again and Thankful looked at himself. "That's enough," he said. The barber grabbed the smock off him. Thankful reached into his pocket and took out his wallet. The barber held his scissors up and sprayed them with disinfectant. Thankful looked at the mail as he walked into the living room; there was nothing but coupons and a bill from the phone company. Sissy was sitting, unmoving, in a chair; her hands were in her lap and she was crying. Sunlight shone in on her through the windows. The day's newspaper was strewn out on the floor at her feet. Thankful saw her and stopped walking. They looked at each other for a long time. The sunlight reflected off of the glass of the cheap frames on the wall. "He's gone," said Sissy, and then she didn't say anything else. As the sun went down, stark shadows accumulated in the corners of the room.

The hamlet of Napoleon looked pale under bright noon sunlight; the long meadows looked indistinct, and the yellow hay fields looked pixilated, and the road was fading into the earth. Some homes, some offices and stores, and some farms, built along the road, punctuated the landscape surrounded by woods and hills. The sky was white. Ash stood in the middle of the road and looked in one direction and then the other. His best friend Computer stood beside him and looked up at him. "Well, here we go," said Ash. "Yes," said Computer. "This is my first challenge," said Ash. "Which way do we go?" He looked down at Computer, who stood obediently by his side and watched him. "What do you think?" Ash asked. "I do not know where the road leads in either direction," said Computer. "Well, what if you had to guess?" asked Ash. Computer thought. "The road leads to the highway, both ways," he said. "And beyond that?" asked Ash. Computer thought. "Another location," he said. "Either way we go, we end up somewhere different," said Ash. "Somewhere other than Napoleon," said Computer. "Any way we go," said Ash. "Yes, if we travel far enough in any direction we will reach somewhere different," said Computer. Ash considered this. "Then we don't even have to follow the road!" he said, finally. "Isn't that right?" he asked Computer. "That is correct," Computer said. Ash stood in the middle of the road, and the bright noon sunlight shone down, scorching the colors of everything, and little Computer stood obediently by his side, and birds chirped and landed in trees or on the telephone wire that ran next to the road. Finally, Ash spoke. He looked in the direction of some woods beyond a wide, sunny hay field, and said, "Let's go this way!" Ash left the road, and Computer followed, and they walked in that direction. "The adventure begins," said Ash.

The field was long and flat; the ground was covered by dirt, weeds, and loose blades of hay. Some of the hay wasn't cut yet but was raked into rows; most of the hay was collected in tall, round bales that sat at intervals around the field. The smell of hay overwhelmed Ash as he walked through the field toward the woods beyond. His eyes began to water. Computer looked at him. "Are you crying?" he asked. "No," said Ash. "It looks as if you are," said Computer. "It's the hay," said Ash. "Oh," said Computer. There was silence, the two of them walked forward. Finally, Computer spoke. "Why does the hay make you sad?" he asked. "I'm not crying!" said Ash. "I'm not sad." "But water is coming out of your eyes," said Computer. "I know," said Ash, "but it's not crying. I'm excited to be finally going, like I've wanted to for so long. I'm happy." Ash wiped his face. He looked at his hands and saw they were damp with tears. "You'd understand if you were a boy," said Ash. Computer thought about that and they kept walking past the plump bales of hay that looked pasty green and yellow in the bright sunlight. "I think I understand anyway," said Computer. They neared the woods. Ash stopped, and turned around, and looked in the direction they came from; he saw a distant car driving on the road. "I guess I'm sorry my parents are so sore about what I have to do," said Ash, "but I'm not going back." He looked down at Computer. "I'm glad you're here with me," he told Computer. "Thank you for saying so, Ash," said Computer. Ash looked back where they came from again, but the car was gone. "I know I can be the greatest," he said. "I just have to keep going until I reach my dreams." Computer was silent, but eventually he spoke. "Yes, I think I understand that," he said. "Do you really?" asked Ash. Computer said, "Yes, Ash, I think so." "You're the best," said Ash. "Come on, let's go." Soon they stood in the shadow of the woods, about to enter. "My dad says there's evil in here," Ash confessed. "I don't know," said Computer. "Will you stay by my side no matter what?" asked Ash. "Of course I will," said Computer. "In that case," said Ash, "I'm sure whatever we find in the woods will be no match for us!" Ash looked into the woods. The trees were tall and grew close together; the dirt floor was covered in weeds and nettles; it was darker than the sunny hay field. "Let's go," said Ash. "I'm with you," said Computer, and both of them went in, leaving Napoleon behind. The trees grew so close together that Ash wasn't sure they were always walking in the same direction. "I hope we make it to the other side before it gets too dark," he said. As they walked they heard many unfamiliar sounds, but didn't see anything except the trunks of the tall trees and the dirt floor. "How long have we been walking?" asked Ash. "Four minutes," said Computer. Ash said, "So far so good! The woods aren't that bad. I'm not scared yet." Computer stayed close to Ash's side. "What will we do if we don't find anything?" he asked. Ash said, "We have to find something. There has to be *something* on the other side of this. You said so yourself." They walked and Computer thought. Finally, he asked, "What happens if what we find is a different place that is the same as Napoleon?" "That won't happen," said Ash, "but if it does, we'll just have to keep going." "I believe in you, Ash," said Computer. "Thanks," said Ash. "I think my parents do too, but they worry so much. I know I can be the very best. I've waited to prove it for a long time." They walked, and eventually heard the trickling sound of a creek. As they walked, the trees were not so close together and soon they arrived at a clearing. "Look at that," said Ash. They stood on the muddy bank of a thin, shallow creek. "Who's there?" asked a voice. Ash started. "Shut up, you dunderhead!" said another voice. "What do we do?" Ash asked Computer. The source of the voices was not seen. "Is it them or just another deer or turkey?" asked the second voice. "I can't tell, but if it is them, you're ruining the element of surprise!" said the first voice. "It must be hunters," said Ash. "We better ignore them and cross this creek." Ash put his feet in the water. "It isn't deep," he said. Computer was standing nervously on the muddy bank. "Ash?" he asked. "Would you mind carrying me across? I'm afraid of the water." Ash turned to his friend. "Oh, of course. I didn't even think about it," he said, and stepped back onto the muddy bank. He leaned over and picked Computer up in his arms. "There you go," he said. "Thank you so much," said Computer. Ash stepped back into the shallow creek, the water came up to his ankles, and he walked to the other side holding Computer. He put Computer down gently on the dry ground. "My shoes are all muddy and wet," he said, "but they'll dry." "Thanks again, Ash," said Computer. "Don't worry about it," said Ash, "but let's get out of here!" The two of them walked away. The clearing was empty; the creek trickled gently, and then a voice spoke again. "Well, they're gone. Way to go," said the voice. "What did I do?" asked another voice. "You gave us away by opening your big mouth!" said the first voice. "I can't see very well. I think it could have been a turkey," said the second voice. "We're never going to be able to catch them!" said the first voice. "We've been trying so long I can't remember why we wanted them in the first place," said the second voice. "We do what we're told!" answered the first voice. "Anyway, I think it was a turkey," said the second voice. "We'll never be able to live down this failure," said the first voice. "I wish we could do something else. I hate being stuck here. I get so bored," said the second voice. "Just shut up! I have to think about our next move," said the first voice. "I can't even remember how long we've been here," said the second voice. "We'll get them, I just have to formulate a new strategy," said the first voice. "I think it was a turkey," said the second voice. "We've seen nothing but deer and turkeys in these woods for as long as I remember." Then there was silence, and the voices didn't speak again for a long time, and the clearing in the woods was empty, and it was quiet except for the trickling creek.

Ash and Computer finally made it through the woods and arrived on the other side to find a hay field glowing under the soft afternoon sun. The hay field was long and flat; the ground was covered with dirt, weeds, and loose blades of hay. Some of the hay wasn't cut yet but was raked into rows; most of the hay was collected in tall, round bales that sat at intervals across the field. Ash sniffed the air when he smelled hay again. "This looks familiar," he said. "It is another hay field," said Computer. "Yeah," said Ash. "But we are on the other side of the woods now," said Computer, "away from Napoleon." Ash smiled, "That's right! Let's go." Ash saw a sprawling hillside in the distance. "I bet there's something over that hill," he told Computer. "It could be a different place," Computer said. "It has to be," said Ash, and they walked determinedly through the hay field. Presently they reached a road; it looked just like the road through Napoleon; it was fading into the earth. "Another road!" said Ash. "It is," said Computer. "I've never *seen* another road!" said Ash. He looked down the road in both directions. "Where could it lead?" he asked. "It could lead to the highway," said Computer. "It's probably just like our road," Ash concluded, "but it's here, not in Napoleon." The road was empty except for Ash and Computer; some birds landed on the telephone pole that ran along the side of it. "Do you think we should keep going and get over the hills or see where this road leads?" asked Ash. "I don't know," said Computer. "The road could be too much like our road," said Ash. "It could be that way," said Computer. "It could lead to the same things," said Ash. "Not the exact same things, but nearly identical things," said Computer. "Right," said Ash, "well, let's keep going then. We don't need a road." "Okay," said Computer. They crossed to the other side of the road and began to walk through the long meadow toward the hillside. When they had almost reached the middle of the meadow, they began to hear a low noise coming from the other side of the hills. The noise was coming from the uniformly blue sky. "What is that?" asked Ash. "I'm not sure," said Computer. They stopped walking; Ash looked at the hillside, he heard the noise grow louder. Ash and Computer waited for something to happen. "I remember this sound from a few nights ago!" said Ash. "I heard it with my parents." "What is it?" asked Computer. "A floating light," said Ash. Suddenly, something arose from behind the hillside, distantly visible in the sky. It was far away, but approaching. It was a flying machine. "That is a helicopter," said Computer, but Ash didn't hear him. The vessel was shaped somewhat like a bird but was much larger; it was attached to propellers that spun furiously. It was a dark machine, brutally elegant. It traveled gracefully through the air, but produced a terrible noise that was all Ash could hear. The roar overtook Ash's senses, and a strong wind blew through the grass of the meadow and almost knocked him over. He could do nothing but witness the machine cut across the sky, briefly above them but then farther away, and then even more distant, until it vanished behind the tall trees of the woods, and the roaring noise faded altogether. Ash stood amazed and he didn't say anything.

Corpus was a hamlet of meadows and hay fields surrounded by woods and hills; it had one road that went through it. Cowboy's farm was an expansive and isolated property that had a red barn, a silo, a stable, a small house, and a wide hay field with a green hillside beyond. In the night everything was dark and layered with shadows. Cowboy sat in the living room of his small house; the light from a silent television bathed everything in colored outbursts. The walls and carpet were sickly brown. Cowboy smoked a hand-rolled cigarette and wrote in a composition notebook open on a card table by the recliner he sat in. In his reach was a handle of cheap whiskey he intermittently grabbed and drank from. There was a calendar from the year before on the wall that depicted a fireman undressing. A hungry cat approached Cowboy but he didn't notice. He stopped writing, and stood up, and walked through the kitchen, and onto the back porch, and looked out into the darkness of the hay field, and walked into the hay field, and listened to the night, and waited, looking into the darkness, until he saw two figures emerge from the distant shadows. Ash and Computer saw Cowboy silhouetted by the porch light of his house. "I knew we'd make it," said Ash. "Have we found somebody to take us in for the night?" asked Computer. "I bet we have," said Ash. They approached and Ash said, "Hello!" Cowboy said, "Hello there." "My name is Ash," said Ash. "My name is Computer," said Computer. "It's nice to meet you," said Cowboy. He looked at them and added, "Come more into the light, please." They walked nearer to the house. He looked at them in the light of his porch. "We're traveling," said Ash. "I understand," Cowboy replied. "We've had a long day and we're tired and hungry. Maybe you could let us rest here for the night," said Ash. "We would be very grateful," said Computer. "I know that," said Cowboy. "My name is Cowboy," he said. "This is my farm." "Pleased to meet you, Cowboy," said Computer. "Is it a big farm?" asked Ash. "Yes, but I'm a solitary worker," said Cowboy. "We come from Napoleon," said Computer. "Oh," said Cowboy. "Where are we now?" asked Computer. Cowboy looked despondent. "Where are we now?" asked Ash. "Corpus," answered Cowboy, softly. "I want to be the best there ever was, ever," said Ash, "so I'm trying." "It seems to go without saying," said Cowboy; he studied Ash silently. Finally, Ash spoke again. He said, "I'm sorry." "You can't afford to be sorry," said Cowboy, "with your vocation." He reached into his pocket and withdrew a packet of tobacco, began to roll a cigarette. "You can sleep here on the porch," he said. "It's not too warm this week and there aren't that many bugs. We'll kick these gasoline cans out of the way and put a blanket down." "Thank you for being so generous," said Computer. Cowboy looked at Computer for a long time, frowning. "Do you have anything to eat?" asked Ash. Cowboy searched his pockets for a matchbook. "Tomorrow," he said to Ash. "Now you sleep, hold on."

Morning sunlight shone on Ash still asleep, damp with dew, on a thick blanket on the back porch of the small house, and Cowboy sat near the restful boy watching him breathe and twitch. Cowboy held a nearly empty handle of cheap whiskey in his lap, a hand-rolled cigarette in one hand, and a revolver in the other hand. Ash awoke hearing Cowboy crying. "What's the matter?" Ash asked. Cowboy started and said, "Don't look!" He stood up, holding the whiskey in his arms, and hurried inside. He came back out holding nothing. "Breakfast is ready now," he said. "Oh boy!" said Ash; then he realized Computer wasn't there. "Hey, wait a minute! Where'd Computer run off to?" he asked. Cowboy watched Ash on the blanket. "Do you know where Computer is?" asked Ash. "He's your problem, not mine," said Cowboy. "I don't even know him." Ash said, "Well it's not like him just to wander off." "If he went in the night the coyotes probably got him," said Cowboy. "What!" said Ash. "He's going to miss breakfast," said Cowboy. Cowboy looked across the table at Ash. Sausage and omelets were prepared, along with coffee and orange juice, and everything was set out on the table. Cowboy sat on a thin wooden chair. He picked up a cup of whiskey and swallowed most of it, watching Ash still. Ash sat awkwardly on a small square bale of green hay that he was provided instead of a chair. He picked at his omelet with a fork and Cowboy watched. The morning sunlight shone through the windows and made the kitchen look warmly hazy. "I guess I better go look for Computer if he doesn't come back," Ash said tentatively. "Why?" asked Cowboy. "Because he's my friend," said Ash. Cowboy swallowed more drink. He said, "Maybe you don't understand that the path you've chosen, to be the *very best*, means you can't waste time and you can't give in to weaknesses. Maybe you don't understand your first failure could utterly end it all for you, and if your stupid sidekick ran off you can't risk losing everything by being a child about it." Ash couldn't reply. "You don't get it," said Cowboy. "It's too hard.

You won't find anything but pain." Finally, Ash whispered, "I know I can do it." "Nobody ever has before," said Cowboy. "I know *I* can," Ash whispered again. "Computer couldn't help you," said Cowboy. "He was going to lead you to bad things, he had to go away." Ash couldn't reply again. Cowboy ate some sausage. Finally, he spoke. He said, "It's funny that we're here together eating a good meal and there's a war on somewhere." Ash said, "It must be terrible." Cowboy said, "The war brings suffering, sure. Do you know why it doesn't matter, not to us?" Ash didn't know. "Because it doesn't concern us," said Cowboy, "and we're safe that way and provided for." Ash said, "I don't understand." "It's inconsequential, you shouldn't, you don't have to," said Cowboy. Ash thought silently, then asked, "What do you mean?" "Where do you think you're going to go?" asked Cowboy. Ash frowned and said, "I don't know." "You have no idea exactly how you're going to proceed," said Cowboy. "Maybe I'll know when I'm there," said Ash. "How?" asked Cowboy. Ash hesitated. "I'll just know like I've always known I want to be like no one ever was, the best, and I'd have to go out and find something or something would have to happen for my dreams to come true," he said. Cowboy laughed, and picked up the nearly empty handle of whiskey from the floor, and poured what was left in his cup. "What do you know about it anyway?" asked Ash. "More than you," said Cowboy. "But you're just a lonely farmer!" said Ash. "And you're just a precocious child," replied Cowboy. Ash fidgeted uncomfortably on the miniature bale of green hay. "I have confidence . . . and will!" he said. "I can tell you do," said Cowboy, "but do you have any direction at all?" Ash didn't reply. "You can't answer the important questions," said Cowboy. "You don't even want to think about them." Ash looked at his hands and saw they were red and scratched from the hay. Cowboy led Ash through the dark and into the stable. "This way," he said. "I want to show you something special about my horse." A naked bulb hung from the rafters and its yellow light shone and dimly lit the stable. Ash stood and watched Cowboy open a pen and let a horse out. The brown animal was beautiful and shiny even in the dim stable glow. "This is Black Beauty," said Cowboy, leading the horse toward Ash. "She's incredible," said Ash. "He's a boy," Cowboy corrected. "Can I pet him?" asked Ash. "Come on," Cowboy answered. Ash reached up, and touched the smooth neck of the horse, and ran his fingers across it, and the horse calmly watched him. "Now then," said Cowboy. He touched the horse's belly. He pulled down his slacks and underwear, stepped out of them. He had an erection; the horse watched intently. Cowboy walked to a metal railing by the side of the pen and leaned over it. Ash gasped. The horse had an erection too, thick and pink, and the horse watched Cowboy as he leaned over the railing, and finally trotted up to him, and gracefully, without instruction, reared up on its hind legs and mounted Cowboy. Ash saw as the creature stuck its muscular pink erection into Cowboy's open anus. Cowboy clung to the railing, moaning desperately as the horse started thrusting on top of him. Ash was fearful and captivated and did not move but listened to the sounds of Cowboy, grunting, being pushed against the creaking railing. Finally, Ash spoke. "Does it hurt?" he whispered. Ash lay in the bed and watched a spider on the ceiling. Cowboy walked out into the hay field and fired his revolver into the ground senselessly. The only light was from a lamp on the floor; it cast stark shadows across Cowboy's face as he sat collapsed in his recliner. He held a full handle of whiskey and his composition notebook. Ash glanced at him from across the room. Cowboy looked at him and smiled evilly.

"The drink!" he said. "What?" asked Ash. "There's not enough to drink," Cowboy wailed. "You're holding a big bottle," said Ash. "I don't *care*," Cowboy wailed again. He opened the composition notebook and wrote furiously. "If only I could defeat existence," Cowboy said. Cowboy sat naked in the empty bathtub with the whiskey. He stood up, and walked into the hallway, and fell. Ash was under the covers of the bed listening to Cowboy breathe, standing above him. The light of dusk shone across Cowboy's body. Ash didn't move; Cowboy didn't leave. Finally, he spoke. "You can't go on," he said. "You have to stay here with me. There's nothing else, nothing to accomplish. It's just dumb pain. You don't understand now, but there's no way you can matter out there. There's no use trying." Ash stayed silent. Cowboy didn't stir; the shadows grew longer. Nothing happened. Ash sat in the recliner; the only light came from the mute television set; silent changing colors moved across his face. Cowboy sprawled on the floor, rested a cup of whiskey on his heaving chest. There was silence and light. Nothing was said; nothing happened. "Don't go out there!" Cowboy screamed, holding Ash to stop him from running outside into the dark to follow the roaring noise in the sky. His arms gripped around Ash's waste. Ash was crying as he tried to pull himself through the doorway onto the porch. "There it is again! Let me go!" Ash screamed. "Don't go near it," Cowboy said, pulling him away. Cowboy sat naked in the empty bathtub with the whiskey when Ash walked in. Bright sunlight shone on them and lit the room. "What's in the sky?" asked Ash. Cowboy was silent for a long time. Finally, he took a long drink. Ash didn't move. "What's in the sky?" he repeated. "Your narrative," Cowboy said. Cowboy turned to Ash and looked at him indefinitely. Ash looked back. There was silence and light. Finally, Cowboy spoke. "Let me pack you a lunch first," he said. He rose from the bathtub, found his clothes. Ash and Cowboy stood at the edge of the woods beyond the meadow. Ash turned around and saw everything behind him, the farm with the red barn, the silo, the stable, and the little house, and beyond that the hay field, and beyond that the hillside. "Here," Cowboy said, and handed Ash a parcel with food in it. There was silence between them, a whistling breeze, birds landing in the trees and on the telephone wire that ran along the one road through Corpus. "Monsters are going to destroy you," said Cowboy; he didn't say anything else. Cowboy and Ash stood next to each other, looking at each other, for a long time before Cowboy leaned over and kissed Ash's mouth softly. Ash walked into the woods and Cowboy stayed where he was.

The trees were tall and grew close together; the dirt floor of the woods was covered in weeds and nettles; it was darker than the sunny hay field. The trees grew so close together that Ash wasn't sure he was always walking in the same direction. He was silent; he heard unfamiliar sounds, but didn't see anything except the trunks of the tall trees and the dirt floor as he walked on alone. When he was hungry he ate his food and left the waste on the ground. The journey was tedious but eventually there was a change; Ash heard the trickling of a creek. The trees were not as close together and soon he arrived at a clearing. He stood on the muddy bank of a shallow creek. He stepped in and the water came up to his ankles. He crossed to the other muddy bank and kept walking. When he eventually made it through the woods he arrived on the other side to find a hay field glowing under the soft afternoon sun. The hay field was long and flat; the ground was covered with dirt, weeds, and loose blades of hay. Some of the hay had not yet been cut but was raked into rows; most of the hay was collected in tall, round bales that sat around the bare field. His eyes began to water and then he began to cry. He walked quickly, ran. He saw a distant hillside beyond a meadow and soon he was out of the hay field and had reached a road; it looked just like the road that went through Napoleon and the one that went through Corpus; it was fading into the earth. Ash didn't feel anything. The road was empty except for him. Some birds landed on the telephone wire that ran along the road. He walked forward, and crossed the road, and walked through the long meadow toward the hillside beyond. As he neared the middle of the meadow, he began to hear a low noise coming from the other side of the hills. The noise was coming from the sky, growing louder. Ash stopped and waited. "I'm not afraid," he whispered. He knew the sound; it grew louder still. Suddenly, its source arose from behind the hillside and was distantly visible to Ash. It was far away, but as it approached Ash could see it clearly: the machine in the sky. As it came closer Ash felt it in his body; his bones shook and a fierce wind swept through the grassy meadow. The wind nearly knocked him down, but he stood against it, always watching the machine as it drew nearer and lower in the sky. Then the roar became all he could understand. The machine was coming down. Finally, it was on the ground, in front of Ash, the propellers still spinning furiously, and something happened: a portal in the machine opened. The portal looked like a metal wound. Ash walked toward it, fighting the terrible wind, and when he looked into it he saw perfect darkness. He said something but his voice was swept away by the roar. He stared resolutely into the open portal; he went into it. The portal closed behind him, and the vessel ascended, and it was rising in the sky, flying straight up, until it altogether disappeared into the atmosphere, leaving the meadow still.

WHITE DOG

In the moments before she woke up, Martha understood she was sitting in the backseat of her little red car, but even after she opened her eyes she had no excuse as to why. This was not the normal location where she woke up, but since it was her little red car after all, and since in the moments before she woke up she understood where she was, and consciously seeing where she was was just a sharply unpleasant affirmation of this knowledge, Martha was not surprised to be there; but she was still concerned because she could not recall any excuse. Maybe, she thought, this is just something that happens. She was becoming unstuck in time, she was losing it, she was losing time, she was finding herself in the middle of things, opening her eyes to a different day with no memory of the conditions of the hours that led up to discovering herself in a new place. A stout old woman passed by her window pushing a blue plastic shopping cart in front of her, Martha saw. "Oh brother," Martha said. She was in an awkward position, uncomfortably folded into the diminutive backseat of her little red car; for a tall woman like Martha, her long legs felt numb after a night spent tucked under the rest of her. She opened the backseat door to her little red car and emerged, and there she stood, seven feet tall, in a red suit that matched her little red car, with a little lipstick smeared at the right corner of her mouth, and she was in the supermarket parking lot, and it was exactly noon.

The supermarket was a large, featureless brown construction, parts of which were plastered with illustrated advertisements for a reduction in the prices of certain food items; people were walking in and out through glass doors that opened and closed automatically. Martha stood there and considered her situation. Without deciding on it, she retrieved her purse from her little red car and then locked the door. She reached into her purse to search for any clues, but she did not find any notes, or even a shopping list, or any other sort of evidence. She thought about it and then decided that it didn't matter. She thought, I must go in. There was no apparent reason to do so, but she thought it and then she did it. She walked away from her little red car across the expanse of the parking lot, step after step, passing two shoppers pushing carts toward parked cars, and approached the automatic glass door marked with a sticker that read ENTRANCE, and the door opened for her, and she walked right in, like that.

There was a woman inside that stood in Martha's way as she entered; the woman looked up at Martha, because the woman was short and Martha was tall, and the woman smiled and she said, "Welcome." Martha thought about this but not for too long. She said, "Thank you." The woman did not say anything else, she smiled and she pointed with a thick arm toward a row of shopping carts; Martha knew this was a silent invitation to take one of the carts. She lingered in front of the woman only a moment more. People have all sorts of jobs in this world, she thought. Some people are presidents and some people stand inside of supermarkets and all they do is say *Welcome*, she thought. She did not want to be the kind of person to judge a person who holds this job, but encountering such a woman right at the start of her day, and considering the circumstances of the particular start of her day, troubled her. This woman woke up early to stand in one place all day saying *Welcome*, she thought. Some people write poems that change the world, she thought. She wrapped her hands around the handle of the nearest shopping cart and pulled the vehicle toward her. The cart was nestled inside a row of identical blue carts but it detached from the rest with a plastic sound. I will not think about that woman, she thought. I have never seen her before and I will never see her again, she thought. She wondered if that was true. She wondered if there was a causal relationship between the first part of her thought, I have never seen her before, and the second part, I will never see her again. She had certainly seen numerous other men and women who held the same job at this supermarket and other stores. She remembered the name of the job was called greeter. Martha's job was called provost.

She did not look at the woman who had greeted her as she pushed her cart into the store. All around her there was produce. She knew she had no evidence that she was here to look for anything in particular, or to purchase anything at all, and she could not think of one thing she was in need of in the way of groceries as she pushed her cart slowly into the store. There were other women around her who were standing by different blue shopping carts and bent over displays of vegetables, examining the quality of the food. Martha decided she should act like the other women. She pushed her cart toward an open freezer display that held many red and green peppers, and she bent over the peppers, and picked up a green one, and held it close to her face in one hand, and scrutinized the surface of the pepper, which was shiny and unblemished. She had no opinion about the appearance of the particular green pepper she was inspecting, she supposed she would have purchased it without comparing it to any others if she had had the need for a green pepper in her life at that time; but she went on looking at it anyway, acting as if she was reading the green pepper she held, discerning everything there was to know about the character of the green pepper, even though what she began to think about was how she probably shouldn't eat every day at the Chinese takeout restaurant down the block from her job, but she had never been enthusiastic about cooking, and cooking for herself alone was unrewarding for her and hard. "That one is perfect," a voice said. Martha looked around her and saw that a homely woman was standing by her side. The woman was looking at Martha and at the green pepper Martha held. Martha was not used to speaking to strangers when she didn't have to at supermarkets, or laundromats, or even at her job. She did not know this homely woman, she had never seen the woman before, but the woman had spoken to Martha anyway, saying that the green pepper Martha held was perfect. "Do you want it?" Martha asked the woman. The woman grimaced and gasped nasally. "Oh no!" she said. "I couldn't ask that." Martha extended the hand that held the green pepper toward the woman. "I want you to have it," Martha said. "Are you sure?" the woman asked. Martha did not reply, but she did make herself smile to try to put the woman at ease so the woman would accept the pepper that Martha was offering to her. The woman responded with a nervous chortle, and gingerly reached out, and took the green pepper in her hand. "Thank you," she said. "You're welcome," Martha said; and then Martha turned around and pushed her cart onward. Martha did not look back when she turned around and pushed her cart onward, but after she had taken a few steps she felt a weight on her arm. Turning around, Martha saw that that woman was holding her elbow with one hand and still holding the green pepper with the other. "I'm sorry," the woman said, "I didn't mean to offend you." Martha was confused and so she said, "What do you mean?" "You deserve the pepper, it's yours," the woman said. "I don't want you to walk off without a pepper just because you gave the one you picked out to me." The woman looked very worried that she had done wrong to Martha. Martha realized what the woman misunderstood about the situation and so she said, "It's all right, really. I was just looking at the pepper, I wasn't going to buy it, I really wasn't, and so you can have it, don't worry." The woman let go of Martha's elbow but her expression did not change. "I'm sorry," the woman said. "It's fine, I mean it," Martha said, and turned around again, and pushed her cart onward.

Martha read some of the signs she saw. One of the signs said KOHLRABI, but Martha did not know what that was. She was not excited by the idea of a vegetable she had never heard of and so she did not stop to introduce herself to whatever kohlrabi was. She pushed her cart onward. She remembered once she was invited to the home of one of the department heads at work and the department head's wife cooked a dinner that included many ingredients Martha was not familiar with. "My wife went to culinary school," Martha remembered the department head informing her. Martha was polite and did not share her true thoughts on that meal with the department head and her wife, although Martha didn't enjoy the meal exactly, because it was so unfamiliar, but she thought that probably made her unrefined anyway, and that is partly why she did not criticize, even though she could have at some time applied herself to introducing herself to all the many kinds of food and ways to prepare food that existed, it was just that it did not interest her in the least, and she preferred having her meals picked from a glowing illustrated menu and handed to her over a counter; she was so uninterested in unfamiliar foods that she did not retain the names of the exotic ingredients the department head's wife used in the meal, although remembering this, she found that she could not recall the name of the department head, or her wife either, but she imagined that that lapse of memory was unrelated to her lack of interest in such things as kohlrabi and other foods she was ignorant of. She could visualize the face of the department head, and remember the specific department she directed, but could not recall what her wife looked like, although she imagined her wife could be one of the women with carts milling about around her. That meal was the last meal she had been invited to, but it had not been so recent that her inability to remember what the department head's wife looked like could be a sign that something was medically wrong with Martha. Additionally, it did not trouble Martha to think that she did not often socialize outside of the workplace, because she was not a friendly woman, she knew this, and knew those that knew her knew it. I'm not a misanthrope, she thought, I just prefer to be alone. Without a strange woman trying to converse with her about a green pepper, Martha did not feel discomforted as she pushed her cart and thought about how she liked to be alone. There were women around her, pushing carts and reading grocery lists, but as long as they were by themselves thinking about their own concerns, and she was by herself thinking about herself, then she did not feel anxious to be in a large, fluorescent public space. She did not think about why she was where she was because as she became more awake she understood that if she analyzed what was happening, she would become discomforted, which is not what she wanted for herself. If she just accepted that she woke up in the backseat of her little red car, and walked into the supermarket, and was now pushing a cart through the supermarket, she would be able to stay composed, and that was what she tried to do.

She had passed all of the vegetables and was now at the fruits. She felt drawn for a moment toward the apples. She always liked seeing the different varieties of apples at the supermarket, but never purchased any because she tended to forget about them in the fresh fruit drawer of her refrigerator where they would stay uneaten until they were no longer any good. She still liked reading the names of the few different kinds of apples at the grocery store. She began to direct her cart toward the apples, but by the time she was near, two women had obstructed her view of the apple display, and she did not want to have to interact with the women, so she pushed her cart past them. Presently she found that there was a tall wooden bin in the way of her cart. She had to turn her cart to maneuver around the bin, and as she was pushing the cart past the bin she saw what was inside. "Oh," she said. Inside the bin she saw many ripe green watermelons. She circled around the bin until she found a little printed sign that announced the price of the watermelons. She leaned over the bin and felt transfixed by the vision of all the fat watermelons tucked in there together. She did not at once understand why she was fascinated but she tried to think what it was about watermelons that could interest her. Watermelons were not something she had had experience with lately but nonetheless she liked the way they looked. She felt that they had a cheerful, inviting personality. She continued to lean over the bin, gazing down at its contents, and tried to remember the last time she had eaten a watermelon. She concluded that she could not definitively provide herself with a date, but she felt as if she remembered at least one notable occasion where she ate watermelon. She actually remembered a time when she was a very young child. She lived with her parents in a house with a big backyard that would flood in the spring, but in the summer she would play on the patio as her mother watched from the kitchen window. Her parents would sometimes serve dinner on the patio and sometimes they would throw dinner parties outside also. She was sure watermelons had something to do with the memory. She imagined fragmented images from long ago: part of the back door that was painted red, her pinkish scraped knee, the hole in the middle of the table on the patio where an umbrella could be inserted, the trunk of a backyard tree, and a white brick from the patio with a single slick black watermelon seed laying on it. She imagined the juicy pink fruit inside of every watermelon in the bin she was leaning over. I'm tempted to buy one, she thought. She knew this desire could only be coincidental, but she imagined bringing something home with her, a rotund watermelon to roll onto her counter and cut to pieces. Yes, she thought, she would take one. She picked her favorite, and she wrapped her arms around it, pulling it with some effort from its place in the bin, as the surrounding watermelons all collapsed into the empty space left by her selection, and then she placed her choice in the bottom of her empty cart. She stood for a moment, and appreciated the sight of the watermelon at the bottom of her cart, and then she moved on.

Martha saw a display of potato chips. She had been slowly making her way around the periphery of the store but now she was near the aisles, which took up most of the space in the supermarket. On the edge of the first aisle what Martha saw was the potato chip display. Martha enjoyed potato chips. She kept a bag at work to serve as a light snack. The bags of potato chips hung from the display. A woman pushed her cart by, stopped, examined the selection of chips, plucked a bag from the display, and then continued on, and Martha stood and watched. Martha decided to direct her cart down the aisle. Because the aisles were smaller, much narrower, than the space she had just been pushing her cart through, she grew more anxious than she had been before. She was more aware of how displeasing the bright fluorescent lighting was and she felt as if the soft music being played over the PA system was somehow sinister. She wondered if anybody even noticed the music. She tried to remember if she had been immediately aware of the music herself, when she entered, or what. She wondered, Why do people need to listen to this incidental music while they grocery shop? She wondered what would happen if the music, which was so generic but somehow important, suddenly stopped. She squinted unpleasantly. She wondered, Why does the light have to be so bright? She was surrounded by soft drinks in plastic two-liter bottles and a variety of snacks on either side. When she looked ahead of her she saw, just as she feared, a woman directing a shopping cart toward her. The woman stopped, and grabbed a plastic two-liter bottle of soda, and placed it in her cart, but then she kept advancing. Martha, reluctantly, knew she had to keep her cart moving toward this stranger. When Martha was thirty, she read an article that suggested most soft drinks were very bad to drink and so in disgust she stopped drinking soda, although she never stopped drinking coffee, and while she figured something like drinking coffee must be just as harmful as something like drinking soft drinks, she was not motivated to discontinue drinking coffee, but contrastively she took no special pleasure in drinking soda, like many people did, so once she stopped with drinking soda she never felt tempted to drink soda again and so she didn't. There were such a variety of soft drinks that they took up one entire side of an aisle. The woman was coming closer to her. Martha looked down into her cart and saw the watermelon she had placed there and that made her feel less anxious. She continued to study her watermelon as her cart approached the other cart that was coming from the opposite direction. Because the aisle was so narrow, both women had to turn their carts a little to their right to allow each other to pass. The other woman glanced at Martha but then she was gone and Martha looked up again.

Martha came to the end of the aisle; she could see the checkout lanes and beyond that the back of the greeter standing at her position in the supermarket entrance. She could not help what she thought next. Why am I here? she thought. What a funny thought, she thought. I suppose that's the central question we're all supposed to ask ourselves, she thought. She turned her cart and weaved into the next aisle. This aisle contained mostly bread and other starches; everything was nearly the same color. This was a nice, comforting aisle, Martha felt, but she did not linger there. At home she owned a bread box that sat on her counter next to the toaster oven, but she rarely used either of those conveniences she had provided herself with, and although she did like bread and liked it even better when it was in the form of toast, she never found herself hungry in the morning, when it is most customary to eat toast, and since she ate out for dinner most days, it was a waste for her to have a loaf of bread sitting in the bread box for no reason. She thought about this. Never in my life have I been hungry in the morning, she thought. She was not hungry even then. She looked at the watermelon in her cart but she did not feel eager to eat it. She was going to save it to enjoy later.

On the other side of the aisle, Martha found where all the meat was displayed. All the meat sat in open freezers in front of a long window on the other side of which a woman with a frumpy perm, the butcher, was walking around in a white apron stained with grease and pink blood. Anyone could pick a selection of meat, which was priced by how much it weighed, or anyone could catch the butcher's attention and place a special order. Martha approached the frozen display and looked down into it. She saw a flat chunk of flesh pressed up against cellophane wrapping as it sat in its own pink juices on a Styrofoam plate. This was how everything was packaged and there were a variety of different kinds of meat. Martha thought that the pork looked least appetizing but was more ambivalent about the steak. She was curious about how the meat came to the supermarket: did it come in larger pieces, which is what she assumed, and then were the carcasses cut into little saleable bits and wrapped in plastic? She supposed she could ask the butcher, but the butcher looked unpleasant and she did not feel inclined to call for her attention; the butcher was preoccupied, anyway. Martha watched her turn around over a counter and begin cutting up something new. What a job, Martha thought. Then she thought, But I shouldn't judge, it's hard to find work, I guess. She picked up a piece of pork and thought of someone. She thought of the last woman she had seen naked. I am probably only thinking about this because of the association between animal flesh with human flesh, she thought. She was thinking about Ann, who she had not seen in six years, but who she had seen naked when she did see her, because they were, for a time, lovers. When they were lovers she thought, This is lovely. Now very quickly she thought, Did that mean we were in love? She shuddered involuntarily. Martha did not think she understood love or romance, but she always let what happened happen, the emotionality of it and the mechanics of intercourse were not difficult allowances, and once six years ago the result of her attitude was a love affair with this woman named Ann, and for a while they were two people bumbling through life sort of at the same time, a provost and a computer programmer, lovers, and Martha thought, Well this is it, but it wasn't anything more than what was to be expected because eventually everything went wrong, and Ann went away, and she did not see her after that, and then six years passed, and for that time she was more or less alone but content, not discomforted in life, and she seemed to others as a well-adjusted, albeit extraordinarily tall, woman, except now she worried maybe how she presented herself was misleading because it could be she had a latent problem as suggested by how this morning she woke up in the backseat of her little red car with no excuse as to why, which might mean that she was not as well-adjusted as all that, that something was happening to her that had implicitly been a trouble, and if it worsened would change the way things were for ill, but she didn't know for sure, she couldn't tell and didn't even want to think about it, but there was the memory of Ann distracting her, making her fret darkly about herself, bothersome even though Martha thought it silly that she picked up a piece of naked pork meat and thought of her. Ann was a nice girl, she thought, she liked making meals, she would cook steak. She put down the pork and picked up a piece of steak but couldn't tell what makes one piece of steak preferable over another, besides the price. She did not feel like asking the butcher even though she knew she could. She did not actually care. She looked at the steak, it was a piece of cow meat, it was a little piece that came from a living thing that was bigger. Ann liked to drown her steak in steak sauce,

Martha thought. She liked to watch a specific comedy show every Wednesday night, but Martha couldn't remember the name or premise. Sometimes she forgot about Ann entirely unless something strange brought everything back to mind. She would get bits of steak caught in her yellow teeth, Martha thought. She wished things had not gone so wrong, not because she began to feel lonely in the six years following the time Ann went away, but because having an embarrassing memory that she would lose and regain was awkward for her. This is no place to be overwhelmed over what's in the past, she thought, this is a supermarket. She thought that, that she was in a supermarket, but then she couldn't excuse why she was there because she did not know. "Oh brother," she said. She put down the steak. She knew it was unclear if she had come inside for any reason at all, there did not seem to be a reason, so she was not sure if she would be able to think of a reason to leave, or at least become dumbly decisive and walk out like she had come in. All the packaged meat in the display glistened as the bright yellow fluorescent light reflected off the cellophane each piece was wrapped in. Martha saw this and thought, I will not think of Ann, then pushed her cart away.

Martha made her way up and down several aisles without paying much attention to anything that she passed. Cereal did not interest her in the least and she did not pause to consider the canned goods because she felt that canned goods were only important when she was hungry and quickly wanted to put something from a can into a pot on her little stove and watch it heat up, let it cool for a moment, and eat it right out of the pot she cooked it in. There was a very obese woman in an electric wheelchair in the hygiene aisle so she decided to forgo it entirely. She found herself in an aisle that had a large display of cosmetics and she stopped to look at them. There

were all kinds of cosmetics from different name-brand compa-
nies for sale, she saw. There was a little mirror attached to one
of the shelves. I suppose this is so that the women considering
the different products can see their reflections, she thought.
They can look at their faces and imagine how different make-
ups, and lipsticks, and eyeliners could make them look beautiful again, she thought. She hunched over, and looked into the
mirror herself, and saw that her lipstick was smeared at the
right corner of her mouth. "Oh brother," she moaned and
thought, This entire time! She rummaged around in her purse
until she found a piece of facial tissue and corrected the problem delicately, after which she continued to look at herself in
the small mirror that was attached to one of the shelves. Nobody happened to push a cart by and see her do this, but she
stopped after a few minutes anyway because she had to sig-
nificantly contort herself to begin with, because of her height,
to see herself clearly in the mirror, and that was aggravating
her back, which was sensitive after a night curled up in the
backseat of her little red car. When she stood upright again,
she noticed all the selections of mascara that were available,
and realized she did not own any mascara anymore. If I bought
mascara, she asked herself, would I use it? She tried to remember when she had any mascara. She was not the type to wear
too much makeup, although some of it was essential. Would I
use it once because I bought it and then never again, or would
I use it enough to justify the purchase, I just don't know because I haven't had any to begin with for how long has it been?
she asked herself. She collected several different kinds of mascara, and examined them one by one, but she was thinking
less about what she could tell about the quality of the different kinds than she was still asking herself if she would use the
mascara in the event that she bought it for herself. It's not

much of an expense either way, I won't break the bank, she thought, but I don't like to be wasteful, I don't like to buy something I know I won't use in the future. She thought about what she ever looked like wearing mascara, but couldn't remember, so she tried to imagine how she would look after applying mascara in the event she bought it, then she bent down and looked at her face in the provided mirror and tried to imagine it more carefully, and then it occurred to her that nobody would notice if she used one of the kinds of mascara in the supermarket; if she used the little mirror to apply the mascara she could really know how she would look, since she couldn't even remember, and if nobody saw her nobody would even know she was doing it. Even though her back ached, she remained hunched in front of the mirror and she applied one of the kinds of mascara, one eyelash and then the other. She fluttered her eyelashes when she had finished. She did not know what to think and couldn't tell if the mascara made her look distinct or ridiculous. What I have to ask myself, she thought, is whether I want to buy mascara or not, it can't be about other people's opinions of me all the time. She thought that was a positive outlook to have, and that if she was buying the mascara she was doing it for herself. It wasn't an expense, but she always hated being wasteful with money. She felt troubled when she sometimes overtipped at diners by mistake, and if she bought something and never used it it would bother her for long after the purchase. Is this a responsible purchase, she asked herself, or an impulse buy? I have to ask myself why I don't keep myself in mascara to begin with, she thought, is it because I don't want it? She wasn't sure. It wouldn't be an enormous thing to pick up here, she reasoned. She knew she was already going to get the watermelon and that was something she hadn't come for, something she didn't need but was taking home anyway. I'll make myself eat the watermelon, though, she thought, and then it will be gone. The mascara won't get used up like that, as fast, and I might forget I even have it and I might let it sit around for years under the sink or somewhere, she thought. Whenever I had mascara before that was likely the story, she thought. She held all the kinds of mascara in her hand, but deciding what to do wasn't easy for her. I shouldn't get any mascara, she finally told herself. Martha replaced all the mascara on the shelf. She suspected that if she bought it the scenario would be that she would soon forget about it, and it would go unused for years and years, and one day she would find it if she was cleaning out her bathroom, and then she would have to argue with herself over whether to keep it or throw it out, and it would eventually become an unnecessary burden for her like it probably did the last time, whenever that was, and besides, nobody would have noticed it if she wore the mascara anyway, even though she told herself she did not have to take that into consideration, but she still knew it was true. "Excuse me," a voice said. Martha looked around her and saw that a teenaged girl with splotchy brown skin was standing next to her. She's beautiful, Martha thought, sorrowfully. The girl was leaning forward expectantly and Martha knew she must have been in the way. "I'm sorry," said Martha as she stepped backward. A fuzzy desire prickled up her spine as she watched the girl. "I had my head in the clouds," she said. The girl did not reply but she reached out and grabbed a small bottle of foundation. She read the label and replaced it, and came away with a different bottle that she seemed more satisfied with after reading the label, and then she wandered off. Martha watched her go. Then Martha picked up from off the shelf the bottle of foundation that the girl had rejected. She studied it and came to the conclusion that the color of that specific bottle of foundation was unfit for the girl's complexion; she returned it again to the shelf. There were so many choices in this aisle Martha could not pull herself away, transfixed by the array of cosmetics that she had never tried to appreciate before, since when she was in need of makeup or lipstick or any such thing that was contained within the cosmetics selection, she would, in passing and without careful consideration, pick what seemed like the most reasonable replacement for what it was she was in need of, as far as she was concerned during her abbreviated visit to this aisle, in haste for she did not place importance on her cosmetic purchases, as evidenced from her decision to buy what it was she was in need of at the supermarket instead of the mall, and she would then carry on with her limited shopping needs without looking back at the display from which she grabbed her makeup or lipstick, and without thinking about that particular aisle or the selection that she had made from it again, not even when she returned home, and unpacked the item or items from her plastic bags, and subsequently tucked whatever it is she had purchased in the way of cosmetics away under the sink where she kept all of her toiletries and beauty aides. She was tempted to again pull out and handle all of the different kinds of mascara that the supermarket sold, to read and memorize each name for each different one, to unsheathe the application wands and examine them all in comparison with each other, and to know everything she could about each one before replacing them all again and continuing on with her day at the supermarket, but she resisted this urge, although it took some time to gather the will to move. Martha was not going to buy mascara; she knew it. She told herself this and was finally able to return to her cart and steer it away, leaving all the differently colored bottles and tubes of cosmetics behind her. When she reached the end of the aisle, she wanted to look back, but she would not let herself. She told herself that something frightening would happen if she allowed herself to look back behind her at what she left. Now she was going to move on. This is the only way, she thought. I'm going to move on with my day, she thought. She willed herself to push her cart forward again and would not look back. "I'm not sorry," she said, but she was her only listener.

Martha felt more anxious. She pushed her cart at a determined pace. She wondered if she would ever be able to understand what was happening to her. All around her women with blue plastic shopping carts were preoccupied with simple tasks at hand. Do I know where I am? Martha asked herself. I'm here, she told herself. I'm at the supermarket. She could not stay here, not forever. Maybe nobody would notice, or if somebody did notice maybe that person wouldn't mind, if Martha pushed her cart around and around the supermarket all day long until closing time, but there would be a closing time, and she was sure it would be announced over the PA system: the generic music would fade out, and all those who remained would hear a bored voice telling them that the supermarket would be closing in thirty minutes, and this would happen again fifteen minutes before they closed, and five minutes before, and then the voice would resonate through the whole building finally as it said that the supermarket was now closed, and all remaining customers were asked to leave and have a pleasant night, and then the bright yellow fluorescent lights would begin to turn off, and Martha would be left inexplicably standing with her cart in the shadows, and some frustrated employee or security guard would find her and ask her to leave, or perhaps ask her to explain herself, in which case Martha knew she wouldn't be able to respond. What is there to explain? she asked herself as she pushed her blue plastic shopping cart and glanced again and again at the watermelon she had chosen to buy. She thought, There's still time to avoid what I'm afraid is going to happen, the worst-case scenario. I'm a respected member of the community because of my position at the state university, I'm the provost, I can't be caught trying to trap myself in this supermarket past closing, but I feel like that is one thing that might happen, why I can't say, but here I am to begin with, and it's troubling, it is. The light was too bright for her, too glib at the same time, too unintentional and brutish. "Oh brother," she said, like a cough. What am I doing? she asked herself, and instantly realized that that could be the answerable question. Maybe not, How did this happen? but, What am I doing? She could not provide herself with evidence to explain the first question, but the other question, What am I doing? was a query that she could answer with an explanation about just how she felt. She wanted to tell herself about what she was doing and be clear and concise and true, and she began to concentrate deeply on this problem, but a full articulation was retarded when she, aware that she had been frantically pushing her cart along without looking up and relying on her peripheral vision to navigate, felt powerfully compelled to regain an awareness of her surroundings, and instantly raised her head, and at first noticed that she was swerving with her cart down the pharmacy aisle, stocked with blockish little containers full of medicine, vitamins, creams, and band-aids, and then consequently was overawed that four yards away from her, obstructing the passage that led beyond the end of the aisle, stood a beautiful white dog. That was a fact. The creature remained perfectly still, looking at Martha, as she pulled the cart against its inertia to stop where she was. She did not say anything because she was not thinking anything, she was just accepting what was there in front of her: a perfectly white dog, taller than any dog Martha had ever seen, with a coat that shined out worlds profounder than the fluorescent surroundings, and with intent azure eyes that watched only her.

Martha was dumbfounded, and she was fascinated, and in the moments during which the big white dog watched her as she stood there, having released hold of her shopping cart, incapable of looking away or forming even an inchoate thought about what was happening, the extraneous music and humming noises trailed off, and the pharmacy aisle and everything else beyond that fell away into a radiant and pure, white cleansing light; and the white dog and Martha were alone in the universe together, facing each other and understanding each other as two miraculously present beings, stripped of all the weight that prevented them from complete actualization, and sharing a spiritually intimate romance for all time. Then, in an instant, everything was back in its place, and they had returned to the pharmacy aisle of the supermarket, and both of them were aware of this, and before Martha could force the first awkward human sound out of her open mouth, the dog gave her one last look with its caring eyes, and then turned and strode away.

Martha stood there for a moment. "Excuse me," a voice said. She turned to see a portly woman with a large bottle of vitamins waiting behind her to be let around. Martha carefully moved her cart to the side of the aisle to accommodate this woman and watched the woman pass to continue her grocery shopping in other aisles. Martha said nothing. She still had a few garbled noises stuck in her throat, but those did not escape her until after she abandoned her shopping cart where it was, leaving the watermelon sitting in the bottom, and rushed toward the entrance, passing the checkout counters and the lines of customers waiting to pay, loading groceries on the conveyor belts, and passed without comment the woman who had greeted her when she first entered, and exited out of the automatic glass door that was marked with a sticker that read *EXIT*, and crossed the sunny parking lot that was cooling down in the midafternoon, and unlocked her little red car, folding herself into the driver's seat, and sat there for several minutes in silence. It was when she attempted to bring her car key from inside her purse to the ignition that she became aware that she was full of half-swallowed sounds, and all of a sudden they emerged at once, lush and weird, tumbling out of her like a prayer; and she then burst out in staggering tears, in a glorious fit that shook her entire body and turned it as red as her suit or her little red car. She had seen a beautiful white dog where there should not have been one, she saw a beautiful white dog, and the experience was majestic, and it had happened to her, and it was hers to keep, and she was going to carry it with her now because she couldn't deny it, she had to accept it, she was going to believe those crystalline eyes were always watching her from then on. It's for me, she thought, and she said, "It's for me!" Everything was exactly in its place this time. Martha wept thankfully and smiled and held her car key to her chest as she rocked in her seat, and when she caught sight of her reflection in the rearview mirror she saw that the mascara she had just applied was running down her face, and this time beyond that she saw something else, and that's what happened.

ACKNOWLEDGMENTS

Impossible thanks to everyone who contributed, in various fashions, to the development of this book. Some of the blame belongs to: The Corresponding Society, Robert Snyderman & Christopher Sweeney, Popahna Brandes, Kevin Killian, Anthony Goicolea, Joel Westendorf, Ben Fama (♥), Johnny Temple, & Dennis Cooper.

O: & thank you, thank you, Joshua Furst, implacably—for everything.

Ryan Doyle May

Lonely Christopher is the author of
several poetry chapbooks and the volume *Into* (with Christopher Sweeney and
Robert Snyderman). As a librettist and
playwright, his dramatic works have been
published, staged in New York City and
internationally, and released in Mandarin
translation. He is a founding member of
the small press The Corresponding Society
and an editor of its biannual journal *Corre-
spondence*. He lives in Bed-Stuy, Brooklyn.